GUILT AND CONSEQUENCES

Gambit Publishing Group™

Lyrics of "After the Ball" by Charles K. Harris (1891)

Library of Congress Control Number: 2019921053

HARDBACK: ISBN 9781734178500
PAPERBACK: ISBN 9781734178517
EPUB: ISBN 9781734178524
MOBI: ISBN 9781734178531

GUILT & CONSEQUENCES

An Illustrated Novel
of
Psychological Suspense

by
JOSEPH JACOBY

ILLUSTRATIONS BY CYNTHIA I. OSASERI

GUILT AND CONSEQUENCES

RE: 1ˢᵗ DAY OF SHOOTING – Stroudsburg, Pa. (The Poconos):

Hi:

We're just setting up our first shot of the day. That's Margaret's General Store in the background. You'll meet Margaret later.

Walter Lassally's shooting this one; I'm the guy on the right. Chilly mornings up here in the Poconos.

By the way, Walter left us in 2017 (he was 90) in Crete, Greece – where he'd shot "Zorba the Greek" (1964) and won the Oscar for it, too.

I got lucky, though – he shot one of my pictures, as well – "The Great Bank Hoax," which is how I was able to dig up this photo to include in Cynthia's illustration.

You realize, of course, that this is AN ILLUSTRATED MOVIE ® Not only are they less expensive to make, we can make our own reality, the proof of which you're looking at.

It's all 1's and 0's anyway. Right?

So I asked Walter if he'd please come back and shoot this.

I never heard "no." That simple.

This is the only look you're gonna get behind-the-scenes, though. When I was a kid I got goosebumps just looking at this stuff.

So take it in – and let's move on to more serious business...

Joe J.

CAUTION

THIS IS THE STORY OF A WACKO. AND A FEW, LET US SAY, that are not of the norm. But I'm thinking of only one at the moment, whom I happen to genuinely despise. I honestly did not choose to make him so important. If truth be told, there'd be no story without him. I personally do not believe that the real-life statistics regarding his actions are all that reliable. Even the noted DNA forensic scientist, Dr. Lawrence Kobilinsky, is uncertain about them (more about this in the Afterword).

I suspect these incidences are under-reported because the victims do not want to acknowledge what has happened to them, given the shame of it; much the same as UFO abductees who'd prefer to stay anonymous rather than risk derision and suspicion of mental illness.

Ultimately, though, I think this story is more about its victims, both male and female, than the 'whodunit' bad guy – who will hopefully keep you guessing long enough so you can get to know the others.

It did occur to me, though, that Hitchcock met *his* nutjob in the late '50s – Norman Bates. *Psycho* was a movie nobody wanted to make, and so Hitchcock hocked his house and made it himself. But what Bates did, then, appears 'quaint' compared to what this guy's been up to now (and who knows who else).

I made a picture back in the late '60s that some people said would land me in jail. Instead, *it* landed in a museum. I'm not kidding. Maybe it's all Time and Space.

Proceed with caution, though.

I'm dead serious.

Joe J.

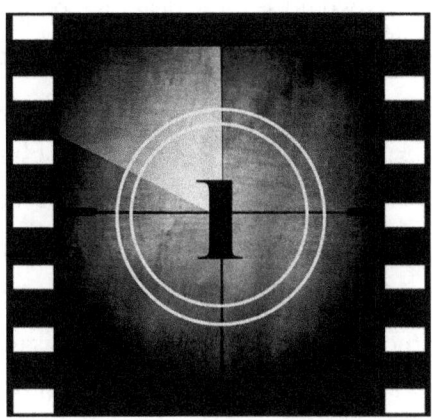

DANNY WAS 12 NOW. AND LIKE SOME ONLY CHILDREN,
he could be rambunctious, combative, outspoken, and competitive, particularly for his mother's attention. Tonight, though, he stood quietly at the foot of the stairs just off the living room arch; you'd have hardly known he was there. This was Mike's Big Night, and what twelve-year-old wants to be left alone upstairs in bed when the adults are having a party downstairs? Permission granted. In many ways Danny was the mirror of his father. Both were attention seekers, but what's acceptable for an adult isn't necessarily acceptable for a kid. A grown-up is *expected* to be aggressive; that's how you get ahead in life, and Mike hadn't missed a beat. Not yet. If you're a kid who's disruptive or seeks attention, you're 'unhandleable.' But if they don't knock that outta ya by the time you're old enough to vote, the same shit that got you into trouble as a kid might make you an entrepreneur.

It seemed like the whole company had shown up to the party, which, in fact, it had. This was Mike's celebration for himself, really, honoring his ascent in DeWitt Media, and with Eloise and Harold DeWitt as the guests of honor, *everybody* showed up—for their *own* good. Smart. Mike not only saw this as a way to congratulate DeWitt on *his* fine judgment, but knew, too, that Sally would seal the deal - a more beautiful or gracious hostess you'd be hard-pressed to find. He'd once said to a successful business friend of his (not particularly referencing Sally, though) that "90% of success in life is perception." The friend grabbed hold of Mike's wrist, drew him closer, and whispered, "No, Mike. 100% is perception." That stuck. Sally cinched it, and she had really outdone herself tonight. Mike was as proud of her as he was of his own good judgment.

Eloise DeWitt, though, was a piece of work. This 60-something better half of Harold DeWitt reminds you of Aunt Clara from that oldie TV series *Bewitched*, that wonderful actress Marion Lorne. She was inadvertently funny and one of those lucky souls who doesn't give a damn *what* you think of her, but not in a mean-spirited way, mind you. In spite of it, or perhaps because of it, she had an intelligence that came through unfiltered. Sally, seeing her brother Joe approaching, made the introductions. "Joe, this is Eloise and Harold Dewitt. My brother Joe's the doctor of the family."

Joe Morris, 60ish, personified exceptionalism; the less said the better, leaving you to your own conclusions; an occupational hazard or advantage, depending on your point of view.

"What branch of medicine do you practice, doctor, if I may ask?" Eloise asked.

"I'm a psychiatrist."

"Are you *really*?!"

"And a best-selling author to boot," added Sally.

"She's better than my publicist," Joe said. "I keep telling her my publisher's paying the wrong person."

"And I keep telling *him* he's too damn modest."

"My, my, such a small world isn't it, doctor. I'm in therapy myself, you know. Have been for years."

"Now, now, Eloise," cautioned Harold.

Mike noticed that something had caught Danny's attention just beyond the living room arch, where he's quietly standing, holding his LOTUS race car, with a direct line of sight to the TV that someone has accidently turned on, without sound. It's a 1918 battle scene from one of those vintage Sgt. York, W.W. I combat flicks, *Over the Top*. What boy doesn't like playing soldier!

Spotting the remote on the rug, Mike plausibly excuses himself.

"What's the name of your book, doctor, if I may ask?" asks Eloise.

"*Multiple Personality Disorders.*"

"Oh, like *Sybil*. I've heard of *Sybil*."

"Well, I suppose it's all the same general area."

Sally takes leave now as well but Eloise goes right on. "You know, doctor, I've been having the most fascinating dreams lately. Last night was totally unexpected..."

"Eloise, dear," cautions Harold.

"They never come announced, you know. I dreamt I was on this roller coaster...and we were going up, up, you know, that very first hill?" ("Oh God," mumbled Harold). "The one with the clickity-clack chain on the old wooden coaster? I think it was the Cyclone in Coney Island. Yes, it *was* the Cyclone, now that I mention it – I could even smell the hotdogs at Nathan's...and then, all of a sudden, My God!—the safety bar, you know, the one that goes across your waist?—was *OPEN*! Can you imagine? Well, I almost died. I didn't know what to do. I couldn't scream, you know what dreams are like, doctor...it's like trying to run." Dr. Joe goes sort of glassy-eyed, nodding reflexively. (Poor Harold.) "But finally...*finally*. Somehow, I don't know how, *somebody* down there musta heard me and, thank god, they stopped the thing. Next thing I knew I was stark-naked!"

"*ELOISE!*"

"One of those naked dreams – again! God, they're just awful; you're just *completely* exposed. Last time I had one of those was in our high school play, and I hadn't even *read it*! And the curtain's going up - opening night!!

"Eloise, dear...."

"Do you think I have multi-plexia disorder, doctor?"

"Multi-what?"

"Am I a multiple personality?"

"Oh no, not at all. I certainly wouldn't jump to *that* conclusion."

Harold's mumbling, "...not so sure."

"It's not me, doctor. I couldn't write this stuff if I tried. People I don't even know show up all the time. Who are these people, where're they coming from?!"

Mike turned off the TV.

"*SHIT*!" Danny unwittingly blurted out.

The room goes pin-drop quiet, except that maybe Eloise has found enlightenment, "Oh!" she exclaimed for all to hear, "Never *thought* of that!" as the room ignites with laughter. Eloise seized the moment to de-fuse rather than display embarrassment, turning with a self-affirming nod to hubby Harold. "See? I told you so."

Sally approached Danny at the foot of the stairs. "Honey, it's way past your bedtime."

"I'm not sleepy yet."

"Now Danny, don't argue with me, you can barely stand on your own two feet." Danny hung stubborn, unmoving. "Danny!"

Mike, embarrassed by his outburst, approached. In a low angry whisper, he said, "Stop giving your mother a hard time and get your ass up to bed!"

"I don't like you commanding me all the time."

"I'll command you, alright. Get upstairs!"

Danny climbed the stairs at his own pace, mumbling, "Drop dead."

"What'd you say?!" Mike yelled, but Sally put her hand on his arm, whispering, "Honey, please. Our guests."

"I'm-goin'-a-bed," Danny dissembled lest Mike misunderstand, continuing his slow walk up.

Mike's expression took on a mild distress; his finger rubbed up and down his shirt.

"Are you okay?" Sally asked.

"Yeh, I'm fine. I just ate too fast."

• • •

Danny slowly opened the top drawer of his chest, revealing a multi-colored toy ray gun with a faux laser. Sitting atop the chest was a framed 8x10 photo of himself and his parents. His sullen expression, though, was in stark contrast to the happy couple standing behind him. He removed the gun from his drawer, his angry eyes riveted to the picture.

• • •

Joe senses something's not right.

"Are you married, doctor?" Eloise asks.

"Huh?..oh..no. No. I'm not." Joe's mind is elsewhere.

"Oh, that's too bad. I have some lovely friends, you know."

DeWitt sees it coming. "Eloise, dear, I'm sure the good doctor does not lack for friends."

"I have an unmarried brother, too, you know. Like my mother used to say, 'Nobody was ever good enough for him.'"

"Eloise. Please!"

Joe uttered a non sequitur in a whisper. "Sally and Jamie are about a year apart, actually. Our eldest sister, Margie, passed early on, sadly.... You'll excuse me, please," Joe approached the stairway.

Eloise, chastened, said, "Oh. I'm so sorry."

• • •

Danny took aim at the photo, the beam "hitting" Mike.

• • •

15

"Honey, are you sure you're alright?"

"I'm fine, really. I just wanna get some Alka Seltzer."

"There's some in the cabinet. Do you want me to get it for you?"

"No, no, I'm okay, honey. You stay here with the guests." Mike made his way up the stairs.

Joe approached Sally. "Is everything alright?"

"Oh sure. He's just got a little stomach upset, that's all."

• • •

Though the light is off in his bedroom, Danny always slept with his door open to capture the ambient light from the hallway. He's always been afraid of the dark, but the greenish wallpaper with its muted jungle-leaf motif somehow made it easier for him to fall asleep. As he lay in bed staring, and hearing the comforting party sounds below, his lids grew heavy. He would not only experience what was to come next as a bad dream, it would also be his first lucid dream, where the dreamer is aware that he's dreaming, and tends to remember it when he awakens. But for Danny it was even more real than that. It was a moment in time when he'd actually fallen asleep and then, suddenly, had opened his eyes (although he wasn't so sure that he'd *dreamt* opening his eyes). And there, standing at the foot of his bed, stood a soldier in full combat gear, including facial camouflage, and his combat rifle was pointed directly at Danny.

With tracer bullets flying over his head, Danny ducked under the covers and fired back with his laser, meanwhile playing dead himself, as the soldier moaned and collapsed. He continued not to move, though, until he'd fallen asleep again, this time for good. But in the morning, he wasn't so sure if he'd dreamt it or not. That's how real it was.

• • •

Mike collapsed that night on the bathroom floor while reaching for the Alka-Seltzer, which is how Sally found him, barely conscious. He passed away next day at the hospital. The moaning and other sounds in Danny's dreams were probably real sounds that Danny had unconsciously incorporated into his dream, serving as content providers or 'triggers' for the story we create around them. It would be great if we could write it the way we dream it! Of course, nothing makes any "sense" when you wake up, *if* you remember it, but that's what shrinks are for. Danny remembered it vividly though and wasn't really sure if he'd dreamt it or not. Maybe Eloise wasn't the nut job she was cracked out to be – Whose dream was this anyway? Or maybe it's just the simple truism, "Be careful of what you wish for in life, you're liable to get it." Maybe they conspire, hand in hand, dreams and wishes. But it was all too real for Danny to forget.

A FEW DAYS AFTER THE FUNERAL, JOE BROACHES

the idea to Sally that it might not be such a bad idea for her and Danny to get away for a few weeks. It's summertime, after all. Joe has his cabin up in the Poconos, which, given his patient load and upcoming book tour, he won't be using anyway, and Danny has school vacation. "It'll give you some time to reflect, recharge. There's something to be said for a change of scenery, just getting away, the act of distancing lets you leave things behind. There's also a camp nearby that my neighbor Bob Sherman owns. I'll give Bob a call. It'll give Danny a chance to make some new friends. Whaddaya think, Dan, how'd you like that?"

• • •

It's a gorgeous day. From Flatbush, Brooklyn, to the Poconos in Pennsylvania is less than a three-hour drive, but tiring, too, especially when you're not all that accustomed to driving, which Sally isn't. Barely a week had gone by. She is even more beautiful without her make-up, a natural kind of beauty, a soft vulnerability, with her dark sunglasses shielding her sadness from the world as much as from the glare of the sun.

Danny sits quietly, scrunched up against the car door, a posture that cries out his own invisibility; he would just as soon melt into the door if he could.

He worries about what happened and the calamity he'd brought on his mother. It had all happened so suddenly though, and in the middle of their celebration. Sally places a comforting hand on his knee. "I'm sorry Mommy."

"Sorry? Sorry for what, honey?" squeezing his knee in reassurance. He'd blurted out "Shit!" and it had even made sense to Eloise. His fingerprints were all over it. But shit happens.

Sally is fortunate, though, to have Joe and her sister Jamie, who has kids of her own. Jamie lives with her husband Jack up in Rhode Island. Sally and Jamie haven't seen each other in several years, and Sally has been promising to visit her. With Danny, of course.

Joe's cabin promises a tranquil refuge, even though she's never even been up here before. She's still, quite naturally, in shock and undoubtedly, in denial; just needing some time, time to reflect and take stock. She hadn't planned for any of this. How do you plan for something like this, for the unexpected? She'd been a devoted wife and mother. Still a young woman in her 40s, she faces the question of what the rest of her life would be like? So many pieces to pick up.

They'd left after lunch and it's just now coming up on 5 o'clock. The remote dirt road that led up to the cabin area is rocky and densely tree-lined. With one hand holding Joe's directions and the other gripping the wheel, Sally revs her car jerkingly up the incline. A dozen or so campers are hiking up ahead, boys and girls, ages twelve to fifteen or so. A male counselor, about 21, leads them. The campers turn as they hear the approaching vehicle, scrambling to either side of the road. Sally slows, winding down her window, and stops directly aside the counselor.

"Excuse me, can you tell me where I can find...Flaghole Road?"

"Sure," he says, motioning to the right, "Right up ahead of you. When you get to the top of the hill, just hang a right. You can't miss it."

"Thanks. Thanks a lot. Is the camp nearby?"

"About an eighth of a mile up, to the left, though. That's where we're headed now."

"Oh. Okay. Thanks again."

"You bet!"

Danny is mesmerized. Who is this girl standing next to the counselor? She's probably his girlfriend, but he's old, 20 at least. So maybe not. Besides she is smiling at *him*. As Sally continues slowly up the path, she can't help but notice Danny's glance back towards the rear window, and thru *her* rear-view mirror she understands. The girl is still smiling at him. "Those boys and girls are your age," she says. "I'll have to see if Uncle Joe spoke with the camp's owner yet; maybe you could join them. That would be fun, don't you think?" Danny hasn't heard a word she said. For the first time in a week, though, Sally cracks a knowing smile. "We'll do that."

As the car slows into the gravelly cabin area, two snarling German Weimaraners came dashing out the front door of one of the two cabins, their intentions seemingly threatening. The growling dogs surround the car. Sally makes certain all the windows are shut and slowly glides over the pebbled ground to the front of the first cabin with the wooden shingle, "Morris Retreat."

Hearing the dogs, a woman in her 30s, pops her head out the side window, then quickly disappears, only to reappear moments later at the front door, yelling at dogs, "STOP!" Their growls become whimpers as they cower, tails between their legs. The woman shooes them back in, apologizing, as Sally winds down her window. "I'm so sorry. They're just a pair of cowardly lions. Hi, I'm Tania. Tania Morse. You must be Mrs. Durant." Tania exudes an overt energy and sexuality, wearing the shortest of shorts and the most revealing of blouses, the kind of thing you cannot help but notice. She's not so much unaware of her sensuality as she is comfortable demonstrating it. Danny is not unaware.

"Hi Tania. I'm Sally. They certainly had me fooled. This is my son, Danny." Tania bends down and pokes her head in through Sally's window at Danny, with Sally arching her back, her eyes open wide and peering unavoidably downward.

"Hi, handsome," Tania grins. "I've heard a lot about you." Danny worries about what she means by that. What did she hear? Who told her?

"Danny, Tania's talking to you."

"Oh, that's alright," Tania says, pulling her head back. "Bob spoke with Dr. Morris earlier about Danny joining us at camp. If he'd like to?"

"Well isn't that *terrific*! Danny – did you hear what Tania just said?" Danny nods a yes. "Danny. Tania's talking to you."

Danny, his eyes cast downwards, whispers, "Yes."

"Oh, that's okay," Tania says. "You must both be very tired. If there's something I can help you with, please don't hesitate."

"That's very kind of you, Tania, but I think we'll be fine." Sally opens her door and heads for the trunk. Danny gets out his side. Seeing three pieces of luggage, Tania offers to help and Sally relents. "Well, if you wouldn't mind?" Tania grabs one of the larger pieces as Danny reaches in for his own small suitcase, and they all go up to the cabin. Sally opens the front door with Tania right behind and Danny hanging back a little with an adolescent's appreciation for the obvious…mixed in with suspicion.

Tania takes a whiff of the place, puts down the suitcase and immediately goes to open the large front windows of the sitting room. "My God we've got to get some air in here!" She pushes the bottom windows up and yanks the top ones down, a whole bunch of gyrations just to get the damn things open!

"Oh, you don't have to go through all that trouble, Tania," says Sally. "I can do it." Meanwhile Danny, appreciating Tania's "dexterity" more than he'd be willing to admit, would just as soon his mother butt out.

"No trouble at all, even the spiders will suffocate."

"There're spiders?" asks Sally.

"Well," Tania jokes, "They're not tarantulas or black widows, if that's what you're asking. Maybe an occasional daddy long-legs. Not to worry, though, they don't eat much."

Beyond the mustiness of the place, the paraphernalia on the walls strikes Sally and Danny both. The walls are garnished with an array of "historical" weaponry. Above and around the mantle are hung several Samurai swords, Japanese armor (Do), Gurkha knives, several German lugers, a cross-bow, even an African blowgun, replete with poison darts (hopefully neutralized!). There were several American combat weapons, too, like M-1 and M-16 rifles, pistols, and more. The overall effect is eerie; definitely unexpected and out of character for the man we've already met – a mild-mannered, studied, somewhat conservative type. This is not the brother Sally's known all her life. For Danny, it's intrigue, real or imagined. But imagined's better. Catching Sally's apparent stunned silence, Tania asks, "Have you been up here before?

"Oh no, no, I haven't actually."

Tania looks concerned. "Are you okay?"

"Oh. Sure, sure. I'm just struck, though, by my brother's passion for all this...I guess you'd call it...unexpected? I'm not quite sure what to call it."

Tania suggests, "How about 'bizarre?'"

"Well, that too!" Sally laughs, defensively at Tania's bluntness. "I can't put the two of him together, though."

"The two of who?"

"Hm?"

"The two of *him* together?"

"Oh...did I say that? I meant the two of *them*," gesticulating with her hands now, meaning the room and him. "*Together*. You know...." She points to the walls. "This and..." seeing Tania's poker face, and finding no equivalence between the décor and Brother Joe, Sally just sort of drops the thought midway. "He's always loved cars, you know. I think Danny must've gotten that from him."

"Well," shrugs Tania, "C'est la vie. We all have our sides. That's kinda what my book's about, actually."

"You're an author?"

"Well, not yet. Hope to be."

"My brother's an author, you know," says Sally.

"Yes, I've been reading his book. Fascinating. We should check out the kitchen cupboards."

Tania leads the way down the hall towards the kitchen in back, passing the stairway to the upstairs bedrooms. "This is pretty much the same layout we've got. I hope the cupboards are bare, though. I mean, it's been a while since Dr. Morris has been here. God knows what's been growing in them!!"

"Tania, you really don't have to be doing this."

"Oh, I don't mind. I like exploring. That's what writers do, you know."

Danny, still in the sitting room, opens a small drawer that has several boxes of rifle cartridges in it and closes it just as quickly. The sudden reality of tactile danger freaks him. His movements towards the kitchen are tentative, like a cat slithering its way through newly discovered territory.

Tania, meanwhile, has been ad-libbing her way through the barren cabinets. "You're going to need to pick up some staples over at Margaret's. If you'd like, I can drive you over and introduce you."

"Why, thank you, Tania, but that won't be necessary. I packed some food for the trip before we left. But if you'll just tell me how to get there...."

"Sure, it's easy enough. I'm sure Margaret will get a kick out of meeting Dr. Morris's sister. She'll probably be surprised he even *has* a sister. She doesn't know, does she?"

"I don't know if she does or not, frankly. Joe's never mentioned her to me."

"There's really not a whole lot of excitement up here anyway. Unless you're a kid at camp! But Margaret's quite a character. Who knows, she may turn up in my book yet." Tania slams a few more cupboard doors for emphasis.

"What's your book about, if I may ask?"

"Well, it's kinda like what we've been talking about. It's a love story, actually. Until they each find out that what they've really been in love with all this time is not so much each other as a *perception* of each other, a projection really of their own needs. When each falls short of the other's perception, and expectations, the relationship fails. What really fails though, is each one's inability to recognize the disparities between these realities, such as they are, and their own needs. In the end, though, they've really failed themselves in not being able to separate the two. I mean you have to know *you*. Of course then we get into this whole thing about who're you and what's 'reality.' Sort of like Lewis Carroll's caterpillar— 'Who. Are. *YOU*!'" Tania concludes the session with one big cupboard BANG! "So where are we?"

This all sounds pretty heady to Sally. "What to say?" acknowledges a sobered Sally.

• • •

Danny, standing at the foot of the stairs now, is looking up at the landing. He's gripped by sudden fear. At the top of the stairs, hanging on the wall, is a WWI combat helmet, covered with camouflage meshing, and combat vestments and leggings, all uncannily like the soldier's in his dream.

• • •

"Don't ask me about reality, though," says Tania, "I heard recently that they've actually found binary code – *computer* code – embedded in the cosmos. You know - ones and zeros?"

"You're asking me?" asks Sally.

"No. I'm telling you. That's what they found."

Tania looks directly at Sally, poker-faced. "So what's real?"

Sally's still working on "so where are we...?"

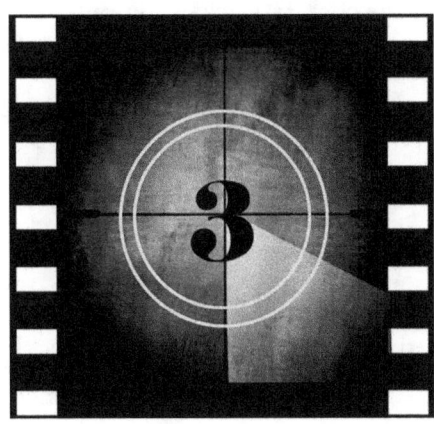

TANIA'S A NIGHT OWL. THE CABIN WINDOW
she'd popped her head out of earlier was actually her writing study. Bob
often spends late hours at the camp catching up on paperwork and the day-
to-day details of running a sleep-away, a camp founded by his grandfather,
and where he'd worked as a counselor himself, in his twenties, when Tania
was barely a teenage camper. The older man-younger woman thing. One
size doesn't fit all!

That night, just minutes after Sally has put Danny to bed and turned
off the light, an aura of ambient light shines through Danny's window
from Tania's study below, gently lighting the sheer muslin curtains of his
upstairs window.

He can even hear the clickity-clack of computer keys through the open windows. His eyes wide open, he assumes it's Tania, gets out of bed, and quietly tiptoes his way to the window, slowly pushing aside the edge of the curtain closest the wall just enough to peek out from behind and look down.

Sitting in front of her computer, she's tapping away at the keys. Tania's tapping just served to heighten the quiet of the night. Being a Brooklyn kid, Danny isn't used to this kind of ambient quiet. He was used to ambulances and police sirens and the occasional argument in the house next door. There is just too much peace and quiet here to get any sleep with. Besides, what's she writing about at this hour? She's wearing the sheerest of blouses. He could see right through it. No bra. And since she's sitting, he wonders what else she isn't wearing, his imagination infinitely more erotic than anything more he might see anyway.

Just then, the headlights of an approaching car pans across their cabin, the way a prison searchlight pans the grounds for an escaped prisoner. Frightened, Danny jumps back into bed. It's not clear, really, why he did this, except he knew he shouldn't be peeking into someone else's privacy. And besides, he's done enough bad things. He can hear the car's slow approach over the crackly gravel, the engine idling, headlights doused. Silence. Suddenly he hears the crickets. He hadn't even noticed *them* before. The car door opens, and the dogs begin barking their master's arrival.

Bob has no idea that Sally and Danny have even arrived yet. Frankly, he's forgotten the conversation he had earlier with Dr. Morris. Besides, the Morris cabin is pitch dark. "Hey Babe," he calls out to Tania. "Whatch'ya got goin', hon?" Reaching in for the dinner bags, and with both arms full and one available foot, he kicks the car door shut. Danny's sure now that he must be her boyfriend. A few more steps over the gravel. The front door opens and closes. Silence. All that remains now is the aura of Tania's work lamp. Danny sleuths his way back to the window, curious. What will she tell him?

With bags in both hands, Bob comes up to her from behind, bends down and kisses the nape of her neck. Tossing her head back now, and revealing the rest, she kisses him back. Bob lowers the bags and Danny's jaw drops open.

He stands as still as a statue as Tania turns slowly around in her chair to face him. Slowly she lifts her hands and begins undoing his belt buckle...

Sally knocks softly. Suddenly stunned, Danny rushes himself back into bed. "Danny? Honey? Are you asleep?" Slowly she opens the door. His closed eyes feigning sleep. Standing over him, her expression is one of concern. Kissing him gently on his forehead, she leaves, quietly closing the door behind her.

His eyes pop open. He's more awake now than before. He turns his head again towards the window. Her light goes out. Again...*"shit."* The moonlight backlights his window now. Agitated, he can't sleep, twisting and turning, staring interminably at his open windowsill when, suddenly, her light comes back on. 'Clickity-click, clickity-clack,' gaining momentum as though inspiration has suddenly struck. Tania's found her second wind.

He's back at the window again. After some moments of furious inspiration, Tania stops, reaches for her cigarettes, lights-up, and reads. A smile of satisfaction crosses her face. The perfect paragraph every writer dreams of. Like a Rubik's Cube that just clicks into place. Tossing her hair and throwing her head back to exhale, she catches Danny's face at the edge of the curtain.

She's smiling at him now, coyly, seductively. An unmitigated exhibitionist, she likes the attention; she's flattered. She's a tease, too, but we know that. Boys will be boys; girls can be girls—an equal opportunity seductress. Danny freezes. He mustn't move now. If he moves she'll know it's him. Stay still. Leave room for doubt. But his fingers let go, and the curtain drops. Now she *knows* he's been spying. She's *seen* him spying. But he *wasn't* spying. He didn't *mean* to be spying. Now he'll get blamed *again* for something he didn't do. She'll tell on him. Then what?

Tania's light goes out.

• • •

Staring into the open darkness, moonlight glow awash his bed, Danny has a visitor. Tania's daddy long legs has crawled up his windowsill and come to visit.

Almost hypnotized, Danny follows spidey's crawl up the window frame and onto the wooden ceiling slats. It must be hard walking upside down like that. Do spiders get dizzy upside down? Danny's feeling dizzy, sleepy too. His lids are getting heavy now, just as spidey finds himself an open slit in the paneled ceiling, disappearing between the slats – and Danny, too.

The moist slatted slats open wide now.

Tania, seductively draped in sheer muslin, is standing farther down the smoky Daliesque combat zone. Her voice reverberates. *"Danny…Danny is that you?" "Yes?" "I thought you would never come. Are you alone?" "Yes. But I don't want to be."* As the smokiness lifts he can hear the battle sounds.

He's carrying a rifle, just like the one hung on the mantel, and trying to run a zig-zag path through a dark labyrinth strewn with soldiers' bodies. But it's hard to run in slow-motion. They're *all* his father, they *all* have rifles, they're *all* shooting at him. He feigns being hit and shoots back. *"You don't have to worry Danny, I won't say anything. I saw what you did but I won't tell." "I didn't! You don't believe me, I didn't. I didn't kill him. I didn't!"*

Sally's hand reaches in, wiping the moisture from his brow, her tone soothing. "Ssssh…sssh." A peace passes over him.

And again, she quietly closes his door.

COCK-A-DOODLE-DOO!

Danny's eyes spring open wide in surprise. He's never heard a cock crow before, not live. Bob and Tania have a small chicken coop out back and the eggs – the best! Tania's been feeding the chickens and Sally's already in the kitchen making a list to pick up at Margaret's.

"Good morning," greets Tania, with some eggs, cereal, freshly ground coffee beans and a container of milk. "I hope you brought some sweaters up. The mornings here are pretty chilly."

"Yes, I did actually," Sally says. "Good morning."

"I thought you and Danny might do with some breakfast 'til you've had the chance to visit Margaret's."

"That's very kind of you, Tania. Thank you. I was just now making my list but I *did* bring coffee!"

"Well," says Tania, "In that case I'll join *you*."

Danny, already dressed, makes his way to the stairs; he can hear them in the kitchen. Bob's already walking out his front door, clipboard in hand, headed to camp.

"Oh, by the way," says Tania, "I spoke to Bob, and Danny's welcome to come to camp anytime he wants. I can give you directions, or if you'd like,

I can make the arrangements for Danny to meet Bob first."

"Why, that's terrific, Tania. I can't thank you enough for all of this. I'm sure Danny'll be happy to hear that."

"I could drive you up if you'd like and introduce the both of you."

"That's very generous of you."

"I don't mind. I have to get up there later, anyway."

Sally hears Danny on the stairs. "Danny? Honey is that you?" Not getting a response, she turns to Tania, "I'm sorry, Tania, would you excuse me a moment?" She finds Danny midway on the stairway. "Honey. Are you okay?"

Tania comes up behind Sally, and calls out, "Hi, handsome." Danny stiffens.

Sally continues, "Remember those kids we saw on our way up yesterday, the kids from the camp? Well, Tania was talking to her friend Bob about you and he says you can join the other kids anytime you want." Sally can almost feel the fright in his face. "Honey, what's wrong?" Danny suddenly darts down the stairs, brushes past Sally, almost knocking her down, and runs out the front door. "*Danny*!?"

Bob's car is just turning toward the camp as Danny dashes directly in front of it, intentionally inviting disaster. Bob is quick to swerve and come to a screeching halt. He quickly exits. "Hey Buddy! You okay?!"

Danny, having tripped, scurries backwards, balancing himself back up. "You missed!" he threatens, as he turns and runs off in the direction of the camp.

Sally and Tania have come running out wondering what happened. Seeing Danny running, Sally cries out, "Danny! Where're you going?!" She turns to Bob. "My God. What's gotten into him? This is so unlike him."

"You must be Sally," says Bob gently. "Hi, I'm Bob Sherman," extending his hand. "Please don't worry about this. He's headed in the right direction – the camp's barely an eighth of a mile down the road. He can't miss it. I spoke with your brother yesterday, incidentally, and he filled me in pretty much on what's been going on and I know that you and Tania have already met. I'm sorry about what happened, Sally, please accept my condolences."

"Thank you, Bob. This is very, very kind of you." She wrings her hands and looks in the direction Danny ran. "But this is not Danny."

"Oh, don't worry about it. I know this is hard to believe, but he'll be fine. Wait'll he gets involved with our activities and meets the kids. He'll be so busy he won't have time for anything else."

"I hope so," says Sally.

"Oh, I *know* so," Bob assures. "Anyway, that's where I'm headed now. Tania tells me you've got some staples you'll need to be getting at Margaret's. You'll love Margaret. Well, maybe love's not the right word. But you'll find her *fascinating*, how's that?"

"I'm hearing so much about her, I feel like I've *already* met her!"

"Don't worry about Danny, though. I'll catch up with him. And you and Tania have each other's number?" Sally nods with visible relief.

Bob sounds like a very secure and stabilizing force. Lucky Tania.

• • •

Morning reveille. Danny hears it in the distance as he runs between the trees of the surrounding forest, an unorthodox approach to camp, for sure, but he quickly reaches the edge of the woods and the expansive campground.

He can see some of the cabins now. Moving closer still, the sounds of young girls can be heard coming from one of them. His spirits piqued, and with nobody in sight, Danny makes a run for the open area towards one of the cabins.

There must be a dozen girls at least, in various stages of morning undress in there. Some are making their bunks while others dress and wash up.

One of the girls is the girl that Danny was smitten by on his way up yesterday, the one who'd been smiling back at him. Almost as if expecting him to appear, she's the first to catch his face at the window and stares directly at him. Her manner is quiet, sensitive, and confident, almost beyond her young years. Danny is smitten all over again.

Within moments, though, one of the other girls, a very round one, spots Danny at the window and lets out a shriek. "A BOY! There's a boy at the window!!" Pandemonium. As if snapped out of a trance, Danny jumps down. A female counselor enters the bunk, and the girls are frantic in their attempted explanations, but she gets it pretty quickly. And as Danny scoots off, she yells, "Looking for someone?"

• • •

Bob's got his feet up on his wooden desk, hands clasped behind his neck, with Danny sheepishly sitting opposite. "Well, I see you found us alright. Not bad. Now, don't quote me on this, because I'll deny it if you do, but I like your approach. Except, ya gotta use a little less moxie, Dan. Ya know what I mean? Be cool."

Danny, untrusting but sensing Bob's efforts, nods okay even though he hasn't a clue what "moxie" means. Bob turns to the large activity cork-board with the daily events posted. "Well. Let's see now: breakfast." Turning back to Danny, "By the way, you ain't had any breakfast yet, have you?" Danny nods a quick no. "Well that's good, me neither." Bob continues looking over the daily schedule. "Let's see here, we have: assembly, crafts, dramatics, photo shop." Turning to Danny, he explains, "the old-fashioned kind, ya know, with a camera. We even have a photography counselor over at the photo shop. Then there's canoeing, fishing, archery, badminton, Ping-Pong, indoor games…and that's just the *early* morning schedule. We got swimming late morning." Again turning back to Danny, "You like to swim?" Again Danny nods, this time yes.

"Well, we're in great shape then. Coed, too, by the way, 'case you haven't noticed. Gee – that's a pretty good schedule if I say so myself. Whaddaya think, Dan?" Danny's got his lips puckered, nodding up and down, as if to say 'Ain't too shabby.' "Yeah. I agree," says Bob, going over to one of the large bins with the camp polo shirts. "Let's see. I'm gonna guess and say you're a medium."

Danny speaks. "Small."

"Gee, you don't look so small to me. I wouldn't wanna mess with you, that's for sure." Now he's got Danny kinda smiling. "Let's see. Stand Up, please." Danny stands up as Bob holds the T-shirt up to Danny's chest for size. "Welcome to Camp SummerSunset!"

Danny smiles broadly.

As they're making their way up the path to the morning mess hall, Bob comments, "Ya know, Tania's said some very nice things about you."

His head down, Danny mumbles, "No she hasn't."

Bob's surprised. "Whaddaya mean, 'No she hasn't'? She has too!"

"Like what?" Danny challenges.

"Well, like she just thinks you're a pretty cool guy."

"What else?"

"Nothing else. Why?"

Danny just lowers his head and nods.

At the entrance to the Mess Hall, Bob bows gently, his arm extended. "After you, monsieur!" Danny smiles shyly and enters the mess, with Bob right behind.

If you've ever been to camp before, you know what two hundred hungry, raucous kids sound like, especially at breakfast! Danny's never even *seen* this many kids before. Being an only child can breed a certain self-imposed solitariness. But he doesn't mind the hullabaloo, he actually kinda likes it, you can tell. You can get lost in this noise. And still be alone. The girls are on the other side, anyway, but he was thinking that if he could spot her (he still doesn't even know her name) he could at least wave. That would count for more than being alone.

Bob brings Danny over to a table that has an empty seat and introduces him to "Uncle" Phil, a counselor, and some of the kids, too. The tables are oblong, so that the counselor sits at the head of it and there are usually five kids on either side, except this bunk is short a kid. While Bob's introducing Uncle Phil to Danny, one of the girls over on the girl's side, the very round one, recognizes Danny and word gets 'round the table pretty quickly. Liza's at this table.

"Go ahead, Dan," says Bob, "have some breakfast and I'll catch up with you later." Danny gets some eggs and toast and returns to the table, but just as he's about to sit, he sees Liza smiling, and even sort of waving, a hand at waist level. He smiles back, of course, returns the 'wave,' and slowly sits.

Mortimer, the camp bully (known gleefully as Fatso), is sitting next to Danny. He's about Danny's age and twice the weight. Well, almost. He's picked-up on Danny's connection with the girl and doesn't like it. Jealous. "She ain't so hot," says Mortimer.

"Huh?"

"I said she ain't so hot."

"Hey, Dan" says Uncle Phil, sliding over the metal pitcher, "How about some hot cocoa?" Danny says okay and Uncle Phil holds the pitcher out to Mortimer. "Mortimer, if you wouldn't mind passing this to Danny."

"Yeh," says Mortimer, "I want some, too."

"Well, you've already had some, so why don't you pass it to Danny first and I'm sure he'll give it back to you when he's done with it."

"I was here first."

Nobody likes him. Even the counselors can't stomach him. Mortimer grabs the handle on the metal pitcher and yanks it away, spilling some of it into Danny's lap.

"Hey!" Danny yells, "What's the big idea!"

"I saw that, Mortimer," Phil's voice rising.

"He moved his cup!"

"I did not. I didn't even touch my cup!" The hall has suddenly quieted down.

"He's too busy minding other people's business," complains a jealous Mortimer.

"Yeah? Whose?!"

"Mine, that's whose!"

"Bullshit," says Danny, as he reaches for Fatso's napkin to dry himself off.

Mortimer pulls it back, "Use your own fuckin' napkin!"

"Hey—watch that mouth!"

Danny pulls it back. "I'll use your napkin if I feel like it!"

Fatso throws a punch! Danny throws one back. They get up, chairs fall back, fists fly. Mayhem explodes. Kids throughout the hall are in an uproar, some are standing on tables. *Everybody's* rooting for Danny! "*Kick Fatso's ass!*"

Danny, though outweighed, is the better fighter – more energetic and nimble, with Fatty having a tough time navigating his own weight, more bluster than throw-power. Uncle Phil, seeing the bully shown up, is almost reluctant to stop the fight. His interference is restrained, almost imaginary, the line between referee and "responsible authority" being somewhat blurred. But Liza, still sitting, is quietly proud.

Bob enters from the kitchen, blows his whistle, and yells at the kids to take their seats. He approaches both boys. The mayhem subsides. Phil is helping to pull them apart now, and holding the bully as Bob arrives at the table. Phil's summing it up, but Bob knows the score. "Okay, Mort. Come with me, please."

As Bob and Mort leave the hall, the kids are cheering "Lock Him Up, Lock Him Up!" Where'd they hear that?

Danny searches for Liza. She's smiling ear-to-ear.

EARLY MORNING AT MARGARET'S GENERAL STORE

looks pretty much what Sally might've imagined: a sort of rustic, three-floored wooden structure, probably built sometime in the 50s, that would fit in perfectly with most Hollywood vintage small-town settings. The General Store is downstairs, the living quarters upstairs. The store's delivery van is usually parked at the side of the store. The 30ish year-old delivery boy, Lyle, is just now hosing it down as Sally pulls in alongside the opposite curb. There's a certain creepiness about Lyle, though—even his smile can feel threatening. But appearances can be misleading and he *is* a good worker. Of course, you'd have to be a bit off-center to be working for Margaret in the first place.

Margaret, a dour woman in her 60s, is loading the paper spool into one of those mammoth, heavy, metal "gold-plated" 50s cash register jobs, the ones with the 'clickity' raised metal number keys and the wooden cash drawer that flies open with the force of a tank when you churn the handle to ring up a sale. A no-warmth taskmaster at heart, Margaret, whoever or whatever else she is, clearly runs the show around here. The beer delivery truck has just pulled up. "Clarence! Beer delivery!"

There are two beds in their spacious upstairs bedroom. One is a single bed, plainly made, up against the corner of the far wall, where Clarence is getting dressed. The second is a queen-size bed befitting a queen, or at least a madam, replete with pink duvet and three fluffed pillows. A beautiful Maine Coon cat, a real one, is spread-eagle in all her splendor, napping. There are a few head mannequins with coiffed wigs, too, plenty of perfume decanters and assorted make-up paraphernalia on the vanity, including, incongruously, a 50s Rolleiflex twin-lens reflex film camera.

The wall above the vanity is crowded with 8x10 black-and-white framed photographs of what appears to be a Victorian costume ball peopled by elegant twenty-somethings, the 1980 senior college graduating class, set in the gymnasium. Also on the vanity are three framed 5x7 black-and-white photographs, the details of which you can't really make out unless you get up close. They were taken in Coney Island in the late 70s or even, perhaps, 1980. Two are of a very pretty girl by herself and one of the girl with her twenty-something fiancé, who's actually taking the picture through one of those distorting funhouse mirrors. A selfie before its time.

Clarence is a quiet, sad, slender fellow in his 40s, who somehow embodies the ethos of an outsider. He's pulling up his denim bib overalls and lacing his work shoes. His solitariness is palpable and his relationship to Margaret obscure, although he appears much too young to be her husband *or* boyfriend, but he's no child, either, in spite of the fact that she treats him like one.

Margaret, at the top of her lungs now, has a way of expressing impatience with bizarre musical sarcasm and a vibrato that could reach the far side of the moon, let alone the upstairs bedroom. "Clarence!! (ala Jeanette MacDonald's *Indian Love Song*) When I'm Calling You…Ooo, Ooo..Will you answer, too…Ooo.Ooo. Clarence! Get your ass down here!" He grabs his workman's cap and heads for the stairs.

Sally, meanwhile, is all smiles. She's just gotten off her cell with Tania who called to let her know that Danny's been adjusting to camp just beautifully, all the kids love him, and Bob sends his best. Sally opens the car door, and walks jauntily across street towards the market. Clarence's hand truck, loaded with beer cases and heading in the same direction, stops on a dime to give Sally the right of way. "Good morning!" Sally greets Clarence.

He is, quite literally, stunned that she's even noticed him, let alone that she's a very pretty woman. He tips his cap, says hello. "I'm Sally. Dr. Morris's sister."

Clarence introduces himself and Sally motions him to go first "No, no, ma'am. Please. You." As Sally passes, he is momentarily stilled, visibly moved that she paid him any notice at all, and he responds sotto voce, "Thank you."

• • •

"Good morning!" greets Margaret.

"Good Morning. You must be Margaret."

"Oh yes…unfortunately, I must be. There are times though when I wish I wasn't."

"Oh? Why's that?"

"Oh, my dear, you wouldn't want to know."

"But I've heard so many wonderful things about you, Margaret. Who would you be if you weren't *you*?"

Deadpan, "Mahatma Gandhi."

Sally is stunned. "Huh? Are you serious?"

"Oh, God, yes. Couldn't *be* more serious. 'Satisfaction, my dear, lies in the effort, not in the attainment. Full effort is full victory.'"

"I don't think I've ever heard that before. Gandhi said that?"

"Yes, and so much more. The outcome, my dear, may not be entirely what you'd hoped, or even in your powers, but it's the *process* – the _full effort_ – that gives meaning. I've spent years reminding myself of this and *still* fall short. God knows I've tried, though."

"I guess I never thought of it that way," says Sally. All she came for are groceries, for God's sake, but has somehow fallen into Margaret's soliloquy. "Andy Warhol promised we'd all be famous for 15 minutes. I never cared much about fame though, my dear, but I *was* a damn good photographer."

"*Were* you, really?*"

"Oh God, yes! Lead photographer for *The Comet*, our high school year-book. I had a Rollie, still do, a Rolleiflex 120-film camera, none of this digital stuff. Did my own developing. New Utrecht High School, Boro Park, Brooklyn. I've got some wonderful pictures upstairs to prove it."

"Oh. I believe you."

"Oh yes, success here and there. But then that feeling of *Now what?*! Never could get a grip on it. Couldn't shake it, either."

"Unfortunately, I'm not that familiar with Boro Park," says Sally. "I grew up in Flatbush."

"*Flatbush*! My God. Why didn't you say so! What part, dear?"

"East 29th just off of Kings Highway. Do you know the area?"

"Do I *know* it?! Like the back of my hand. I had many friends who lived in Flatbush. Flatbush was a hotbed back in the day, ya know—Woody Allen came from Flatbush. Streisand, too, did you know that?

"I think I'd heard that, actually," says Sally. "I also went to Brooklyn College."

"*Brooklyn Col*—!" —Stunned, Margaret just looks at her, then suddenly realizes the awkwardness of her silence. "You'll have to forgive me. I studied photography at Brooklyn. Only for a semester, though. Had to drop out. Family matters."

"I understand," says Sally.

"Oh well, it's such a small world, isn't it, dear? Sadly, it all comes and goes too quickly. Even the movies...*disappear* – the old Vitagraph Studios. History. *History*! - Right there on Avenue M. Of course, this does go back a way, even before *my* time, thank God. Oh, What the hell's time any-way? Einstein did say linear time was an illusion, you know - although a persistent one." Margaret still can't help staring at Sally, as if she'd just dropped in from Mars. Sally took no notice. "Who'd've guessed, though? I'm just an old fogey name-dropper anyway. '*A Tree Grows in Flatbush*.'

Great movie.... No, that's not right."*

"It *grew* in *Brooklyn*, though, didn't it? Well...Flatbush *is* Brooklyn, and Brooklyn was the whole wide world. Oh! Who cares?! Those trees—those glorious Flatbush trees are what I remember most. Boro Park was concrete—blocks and blocks of concrete—that part I knew all too well. I'll bet if you asked any of these celebrities, though, they'd tell you the same damn thing: It's the *now whats?* that are out to get ya. Every time! Can't leave well enough alone. Nothing's *ever* enough: *Now what*!? I suppose it's a blessing, though. Anything that'll keep you distracted is a blessing."

"Distracted from what?" asks Sally.

"*Death*, dear. Just a lot of running around to keep your mind off of it." 'Full *effort* is full victory.' There's no other answer, really." Margaret beckons Sally to lean in closer, whispering, "I finally figured it out...it's all bullshit. You're stuck with the *now whats* 'til you drop. Nothing's *ever* going to be enough."

Sally straightens up now, not so much in shock, as in calculated response to the rightness of Margaret's conclusion...and *anything* to get to the groceries. "Makes sense to me," says Sally.

"...Oh I've *so* enjoyed our tete-a-tete,"says Margaret, "May I ask who

. . . .

* Margaret's got it all screwed up. The film she's talking about *is* "*A Tree Grows in Brooklyn*," *not* Flatbush, directed by Elia Kazan. It was before her time anyway. If she was a photographer on *The Comet*, New Utrecht High School's yearbook, then that puts her in Boro Park at least as a teenager (the "concrete" part she nails cold, that part even *I* remember). But having lived in several sections of Brooklyn myself, including Flatbush, I can attest to her fond memories of those magnificent tree-lined streets. And while she presumably took courses in photography at Brooklyn College, she admits to being something of a 'name-dropper,' acknowledging, however, that she never knew either Mr. Allen or Ms. Streisand. But I do understand her reach for inclusion. Whatever vestiges of fame she might've clung to, and may still, even if only through the thinly veiled association of having once lived in their neighborhood, let her have her trees.

I've had the pleasure of speaking with?"

"Oh, I'm sorry. I'm Sally. Sally Durant. Dr. Morris' sister."

Margaret is stilled. "I never knew he *had* a...I mean...."

"Oh yes," injects Sally, "More than one, in fact. My sister Jamie lives up in Rhode Island." Margaret is quietly but visibly moved. Something is just not being said, though. Visibly touched for some reason, she looks deeply into Sally's face. "Yes, I can see that, actually...my God."

Lyle, the delivery boy, holds the door for Clarence's hand-truck with its beer load.

"Well! It's so lovely meeting you, Sally. Now—what can we help you with?"

Sally takes out her shopping list. Clarence is just now passing behind her with his hand truck.

"Rather than my rattling off these items...," Sally suggests, and hands Margaret her list. "If you'd prefer to box them in whatever sequence is easiest for you, I'll just check out your magazine rack. My car's parked just across street."

"Splendid," says Margaret. "Clarence, I'm going to need your help back here, please."

As Margaret and Clarence go about their business filling her order, Sally peruses the rack. Margaret, glancing over, is visibly struck by her pensive pose as she examines the magazines. Sally holds her forefinger to the bridge of her nose, her thumb just under her chin. Margaret *knows* that pose.

For Sally, though, there's something disquieting about Lyle. He's been leaning on the counter over by the door there, staring at her from the moment she walked into the store. The few moments when she's felt his presence and glanced over, he breaks into a weird tight-lipped crooked grin.

"You know Sally," Margaret says, "I can have Lyle deliver these to the cabin if you'd like. There's no charge; there's no need to wait."

"Oh no, that won't be necessary, I'm right across street," Sally says as she lifts the morning paper and a few magazines from the rack. "And if you would just add these in please," she says, feeling she can't get out of there fast enough. Meanwhile, Clarence is working on her second box. Sally's ordered more than she realized. "Is that all mine?"

"Oh yes," says Margaret, "almost done, though. One more box should do it." She reads off the remaining items to Clarence. "I just hope you'll be able to handle these on the other end, though. They are a bit heavy," and says, just confidentially, "Lyle's very efficient. You really don't have to tip him very much. Delivery's free, you know. But that's up to you, of course."

Sally's feeling like a two-bit cheapskate with her sudden realization that the poor guy, no matter what she's thinking, probably survives on tips. "Well, okay then. If he could follow behind me that would be fine."

"Lyle! Miss Durant is going to be headed back to Dr. Morris' cabin. Would you please…" Lyle comes over, lifts the cartons, one at a time and takes them to the van.

Sally asks how much she owes, and Margaret turns to her cash register. "Well, let's see now…." She does her clickity-clackity register routine, which, in and of itself, is performance art worth the price of the groceries. "How is the good doctor? I haven't seen him in months."

"He's fine, thank you. He's just been very busy, you know."

"Oh yes, of course. And he's a famous author now, too, let's remember." Margaret reaches below and pulls out a dog-eared copy of his book under the counter. "You might say I've been reading up a bit. Who would've guessed, though…I mean, I might've but…I didn't. I never even met the family. Except now for you, of course. It's been very nice to meet you, Sally. I've been wanting…I've been *waiting*…." It's not like Margaret to stumble over her words. "I should say," straightening herself up, "I would love to get him to sign this."

"I'm sure he'd be delighted to," says Sally.

"Well," says Margaret, "I guess that's the price of success, isn't it? Being busy, I mean. Nothing wrong with busy. Keeps you young! Still can't say I really *know* him, though. Who really knows anyone? I'm not even sure *I* know *me*! Why don't we exchange numbers? This way you can just pick up the phone anytime you'd like and save yourself a trip."

As they exchange contact numbers, Sally can't help but notice that Margaret has rings on every finger. Most are garish, except for one that appears to be a simple gold wedding band.

Sally's ride back to the cabin is uneventful enough except for the lingering worry that the guy following behind her is some kind of a nut-job. But no matter what she's feeling, he works for Margaret for God's sake, and she's got a business to protect, and that's that. "Chill, Sally. Chill."

That's what she keeps telling herself. Maybe if she says it enough she'll believe it. It's like the ones and zeros Tania was talking about. So if nothing's real, what's to worry?

• • •

Sally took her newspaper, but she left her magazines on the counter. Margaret is still standing near the register looking at Dr. Morris's author photograph in a way she hasn't looked before. He's a much younger man in the photo; author pictures sometimes are though, although no one's likely to mistake Dr. Morris for a sex symbol. Margaret appears to be straining for some kind of memory, something that Sally's triggered. Could they have met earlier? And even if they had, so what? He's not her type anyway, not even the young version. Margaret's been up here for almost thirty years now. Dr. Morris can't have been here for more than ten. Margaret remembers when old man Ferleger kicked the bucket. That was just about ten years ago, and then his family sold the cabin to Morris. They're about the same age, though. None of this would ever have been triggered had Sally not walked in.

Margaret turns now and looks down at the floor behind her: total dishevelment, boxes strewn all over the place. Nothing pisses her off more than disorder, a disorder exacerbated by her present state of perplexity. Life has enough disorder without adding to it. "Clarence! Where the hell did that boy go? I want you to get your ass back down here and clean up this mess!" Suddenly, she slips on a piece of shiny white cardboard, her head's thrown back, her wig flies off, and she lands flat on her ass...*Bam*!

What the hell have we got here?!

IT'S ONE OF THOSE OLD 78 RPM VICTROLA PHONO-

graphs from the 40s that sits on a nightstand across from Clarence's bed.

His hand reaches in now and carefully drops the needle onto the spinning shellac resin disk from back in the day. The record is so brittle, in
fact, that to drop it would cause it to splinter into shards. The fact that
it survives at all speaks to the care it's been given, but it's been played so

many times that you can hardly hear the lyrics through the scratches. The melody, written in 1891, is haunting. It's become both Margaret's and Clarence's touchstone. Even through the record's scratchiness, its heartfelt story casts a spell.

She's downstairs listening, he's sure. Not much more is needed to quiet her. It's as if Clarence has sought refuge from her onslaught, knowing this will protect him, as if *he* were the cat, now in safe hiding. But our Maine coon, awakened from her slumber, jumps atop Margaret's vanity, and with the nonchalant metronomic swish of her tail, swipes at each of the three 5x7 framed pictures as they fall down one by one, face down.

Clarence carefully lifts and dusts each, putting them back in their proper stance. And with each dusting, a piece of a mystery unfolds....

• • •

"I had a sweetheart, years, years ago.
Where she is now, pet, you will soon know.

List' to the story, I'll tell it all.
I believed her faithless after the Ball."

A pretty 20ish young woman of the 80s generation, is happily swallowing a Nathan's Famous Coney Island Hot Dog, mustard running down both sides of her mouth.

The combination of lyrics and melody spins a haunting tale, told from a man's point-of-view. Though it feels like a story told more than a century ago (and probably a true one, at that), it's as universally now as it was then. How this finds resonance for Clarence and Margaret, God only knows.

In the second photo over, the woman is standing in front of Coney Island's famous landmark roller coaster, the Cyclone, built in 1927 and still extant at this writing.

"Long years have passed child, I have never wed
True to my lost love, though she is dead.
She tried to tell me, tried to explain
I would not listen pleadings were vain."

Oblivious to the person taking the picture, the woman is studying a guide map of sorts, her forefinger to the bridge of her nose, her thumb just under her chin, in contemplation. It's not Sally, though. It can't be Sally. Sally's in her 40s. This was taken no later than the early 1980s.

Clarence is waltzing now with the cat, lost in his ruminations.

And finally the third photo, before the Funhouse Hall of Mirrors....

"One day a letter came from that man.
He was her brother, the letter ran.
That's why I'm lonely, no home at all,
I broke her heart, pet, after the ball."

The man is looking down now, both their faces distorted. With his right hand on the shutter, he snaps them both, his left hand resting gently on her slightly pregnant belly, both laughing and clearly in love.

"After the ball is over, after the break of morn,
After the dancers' leaving, after the stars are gone,
Many a heart is aching, if you could read them all –
Many the hopes that have vanished after the ball."

"Clarence! *Get your ass down here. Dammit!*"

Quiet. Except for the repetitive loping of the phonograph needle.

• • •

Standing at the front door now, her back literally up against the wall, Sally gives room for Lyle to enter, laden with the first of her three boxes, and pointing him in the direction of the kitchen down the hall.

His movements are painfully lugubrious. Still anxiety-wrought, and with 2 boxes to go after this, she extends her hand with a ten-dollar bill. "Thank you very much, Lyle. This is for you. I've got to tend to some matters upstairs now, if you wouldn't mind closing the door behind you when you leave."

With the slip of the bill into the palm of his hand, Lyle courteously responds, "Thank you, ma'am. I'll do that." It's the first time he's spoken, actually. Doesn't sound at all threatening.

As he continues his slo-mo pace towards the kitchen, Sally follows a few feet behind, wanting to shove him along just so she can get up those damn stairs, and as soon as she does, it's two steps at a time, a svelte body in great shape. Her front bedroom, such as it is, has a queen-sized bed, a chest of drawers, a vanity, a few chairs and a writing desk. There're some throw rugs on the otherwise bare wooden floor and three windows, one on the same side as Danny's, overlooking Bob and Tania's. Sally's room is at the front of the cabin. She has a large front window and one on the opposite wall where you can see the road leading up to the cabin enclave. All the windows are curtained. The bedroom door is reasonably insecure. It's one of those old-fashioned skeleton key locks and a simple brass slide-bolt latch on the inside of the door.

Sally is stilled. She's listening carefully now to Lyle's goings-on in the kitchen. She can hear shuffling Lyle putting a box on the table. She spots the skeleton key on top of the desk, goes for it and bolts both locks just in case, taking her cell from her purse, also just in case. With each move, now, a sort of *now what?* kicks in – not that Margaret had any idea of what she was planting, but she did say that death itself was the only *real* answer and all the rest was bullshit and Sally's hearing it all over again and wants to get as many *now whats* in as possible, given the alternative. This is no time to throw caution to the wind. Grasping the chest with both arms, now, she jiggles it away from the sidewall, gets behind it and pushes it right up against the door. Lyle meanwhile, who is just leaving for box number two, hears the scraping noises above and can't imagine what she's up to. He shrugs and heads for the van.

Given what Sally's been through over this past week, it's amazing she's handled things as well as she has, and so her paranoia here, if that's what it is, is understandable. Again she falls still, sitting now at the foot of the bed, quietly listening. She can hear him now walking towards the front door, which he closes behind him. What else can she do? Bed's too big to move but there's the desk and a couple of chairs. She did exchange numbers with Margaret. If he tries to get through this mountain of stuff, it'll buy her time to call Margaret, who could then quickly call the local police. She hears the metallic sound of the back door of the van opening and closing. He's coming back now with box number two, or maybe he's got 'em both, one on top of the other; they're small enough.

A few moments of silence go by.

Sally's literally holding her breath, hearing him slowly trudging down the hall again, dropping the box or boxes onto the kitchen table. One more? *Maybe.* God, she's thinking, I've never known anyone to move this slowly; it's interminable. This time we hear the thud of the front door closing. And then—*Engine ignition*! She was right! He took them both. Her first deep sigh of relief. And then the gravelly sounds of the delivery van backing up and turning around. Sally goes to the far left window in anticipation. It looks out on the road to the cabin area. She gently pushes aside the sheer muslin curtain, just enough to peek through and see the van leaving.

And there goes the van, "Margaret's General Market" painted in gold lettering right on its side. He's gone. 'Good riddance to bad rubbish!' To say that her entire being deflates with relief would be an understatement.

Her adrenalin sapped, Sally just flops herself back down onto the bed, exhausted. Lifting her head momentarily and looking at the foolishness of her barricade, as if someone else had just done this, she mumbles, "My God. What's wrong with me?" Slowly, after just a few more minutes of re-charging, Sally pops back up and begins the daunting process of returning everything to its place. But looking down now at the scraped floorboards, she's thinking, 'Oh crap, look what the hell I've done. Thank God it's not a B&B!' The choice between even more scrapes and not getting everything back in its place is no choice. Gathering whatever energy she can muster, Sally slowly pulls it all back, with the chest being last. She'll explain to Joe that she tried re-arranging things but hadn't really thought through the consequences of damaging the floorboards, given the weight of the pieces, and by then the damage was done and she'll offer to pay to have it re-sanded. There's just no good way to explain this foolishness and, besides, it could've been worse.

But she had trusted her instincts, as her father had always taught his children to do (especially when they coincided with *his* needs) and she'd do it again. Well, maybe she'd leave off the last part, *his* needs be damned. But as she's thinking through this apologia/defense, things are straightened out. Besides, thank god she's in good enough shape to dig herself out.

She can't wait to get down to the kitchen, though, and put some of that fresh Margaret mocha to work. Gathering herself, she turns around to check things out one last time. She's almost feeling a sense of accomplishment, notwithstanding her disgust with herself as she looks just once more. Then, relieved, she spins around, unlocks the door....

...And *WHAMMO*!

Foolishly, she hadn't thought of this.

• • •

"Ready?!" signals Danny.

Liza is dog-paddling and sort of listing to the left with one hand under the water, working on something or other, and the right hand high, compensating. "Okay. Ready!" says Liza, straightening herself up with one hand still submerged, her swim cap in place; her nose clip about to be. Danny, hand to his nose, is ready to go under. "One..., two..." Liza takes a deep breath, *"Three!"* And under!

They're both stark naked, each holding their bathing suits, eyes wide open, deciding whether to breathe or just stare, the undulating surface water refracting sunlight from above. To breathe or not to breathe. Amazing how little air you need at a time like this.

• • •

"*Take it off!*" the muffled male voice demands as Sally backs off to the foot of the bed. She can't go any further. "Please. What is it you want?" He's wearing a full-headed mask, just slits for eyes. "You can have whatever you want," she pleads. He's maybe 5'9", wearing a dark non-descript jacket, medium build, and the guttural voice of an angry man. His weapon is himself.

"Take it off!" She does not know this man. "I said, TAKE IT OFF!" Sally unzips the back of her dress. "Let it drop." She mumbles, "Please, no," as her dress falls to the floor. The resignation is in in her voice. "Very nice," he says. Pointing to her bra, his tone now softer, "Remove it please." Sally unclasps it. "Let it fall," he whispers. It drops, *Oh god*. His gloved hands reach in to caress her breasts.

Sally has left the building.

• • •

Gasping for breath, Liza and Danny pop up just in the nick of time. As with all summer camps, and especially with swimming, a strict buddy system is in place. So when the swimming counselor blows her whistle and calls "buddy up" the kids grab hold of their buddy's hand, raise them above their heads, and the counselor makes a body count. But when she gets to our voyeur duo here, Liza, unknowingly, is holding up her bathing suit as well. "Oh my," smiles the counselor.

• • •

Sally is prone, face down on the bed. His gloved hands tie her ankles to the bedposts. Now for the hands. He opens his belt while she clutches the railings on either side, her ankles tearing against the knotted rope. She needs to get to her ringing cell that's sitting within inches on the bedside table. Her fingers can barely reach as his gloved hand reaches in and swipes it to the floor.

Slowly he lowers himself on top of her. That's all she'll remember. It's as if the lights went out.

GO TO BLACK.

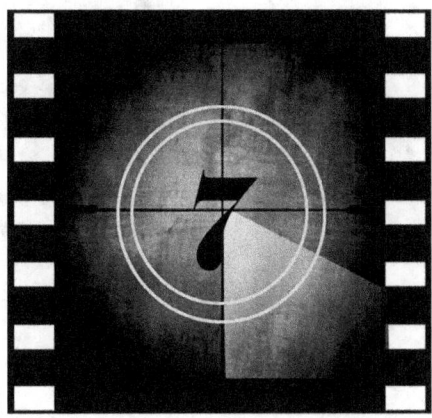

IT'S ABOUT 7:30 NOW. A MORE BEAUTIFUL SUMMER
sunset would be hard to imagine. Idyllic. Both cabins are enveloped by a
haunting serenity accompanied by chirping birds, from the hummingbird
to the blackbird. They're all here, as are the chirping crickets and katy-
dids. A cacophony of tranquility.

The front door of the cabin is open, though. She'd asked Lyle to close it
behind him. He said he would and she'd heard it lock. The one thing she'd
been focused on were the sounds; she had no visual clues anyway. Besides,
she saw him driving behind her on the way up, and he was alone.

Suddenly, an antique of a car approaches the cabin area, looking and
sounding like something out of the Roaring 20s. It is, in fact, a Ford Model A Roadster. Whoever owns this thing has a few bucks.

Ignition off. It's Margaret. Looking out her side window, she can see
that the front door of the Morris cabin's half open. Leaning behind her is
Clarence, who has a way of disappearing in plain sight. "Now just wait for
me here, and if I need your help I'll call for it, God help me." Margaret, the
magazines under her arm, heads for the open door. "Hello-o-o? Anybody
home? It's just me, Margaret!"

Nothing. Total silence. It's so eerily quiet, in fact, that she's wondering when the boom's gonna drop. Not one to be forestalled, Margaret enters the hallway. She's actually never been inside Dr. Morris' cabin before, and with the setting sun shining through the windows, chirping critters and nothing moving, it all feels very surreal. The kitchen down the long hallway is so bright with ambient light that even the table and chairs seem smothered to the point of ghostly white invisibility. Very Kubrickian. Margaret thinks she sees a pair of legs sitting there, though. "*Hel-l-lo.* It's Mar-ga-ret. Is that you, Sally?" She figures where there're legs there's probably a person—but she has to admit, they're gorgeous gams. Total silence. Margaret mumbles, "Maybe I've lost it altogether."

As she makes her way slowly down the hallway, she can't help but take in the paraphernalia that comes with it. "How strange," she mumbles. "Not at all what I'd imagined." But the legs are real, indeed. Finally stopping at the kitchen archway, and seeing Sally seated in the chair, seemingly stranded somewhere in space; staring at the wall, three pieces of luggage at her side, Margaret clears her throat and says with mild embarrassment,

"Good evening."

Sally just looks up at her, not a blush, and speaks in a distant mono-tone. "Oh. Hi. I'm sorry. Have you been standing there long?"

"No. I just saw the door was open and I...."

"Oh, please, please come in."

"Well," says Margaret, "I really didn't mean to be barging in on you like this, but you did forget these magazines, you know."

"Did I really? I'm so forgetful these days, aren't I? Thank you." Sally motions Margaret to sit, but Margaret can't help but feel Sally's trance-like disconnect. "Please. Make yourself comfortable. I was just sitting here lost in thought, really."

"Yes," says Margaret, "You're very convincing. Your thoughts have a way of speaking for themselves." Margaret feels Sally's unease. "Oh well. I just wanted to deliver these and make sure everything was okay. That's all. I did try calling, you know."

Sally suddenly turns and looks at Margaret. "No. No I didn't know that."

"Oh yes. Yes, I did. At first I thought we'd been disconnected and then when I tried again there was no answer, except for your message. So I just thought I'd come up to see if anything was wrong."

"Wrong?" asks Sally.

On the one hand, Sally is responsive and coherent. But her face and demeanor betray her traumatic shock. Margaret has no way of knowing, of course. How could she? She just met Sally a few hours ago but clearly senses this is not the same Sally. "Well, you know. Just an old woman's rusted intuition. Just wanting to make certain everything was okay, though, that's all. Well, perhaps next time on the coffee then."

"Coffee?" asks Sally. "Did I mention coffee?"

"No, I did."

"Oh. Of course. Please. Please sit down. Don't leave yet. At least let me make us some of your coffee."

"Oh, well—if you *insist*. That is very gracious of you, Sally," she says, pulling up a chair. "I can always use an after-hours picker-upper, and a tad of good conversation. I so enjoyed our conversation earlier today, you know."

As Sally slowly and mechanically rises and goes to the sink to draw water for the coffee, she's looking out the kitchen window directly onto the backyard area between the two cabins. Several garbage cans are sitting off to the side. Tania's two dogs are sniffing the cans, one in particular, as they begin circling it like hungry wolves. Sally watches the dogs and worries, but to escape any worry she begins an almost automatic soliloquy. "Well. I'll be back, I'm sure. My plan is to get some of my personal matters in order first, and then perhaps take a month or two off just to unwind."

Margaret is stunned, taking note of the luggage. "You mean you're leaving us? But you've only just come up!"

Sally's increasingly fearful of the dogs. "Things don't always go the way we've planned them to, do they? There's bound to be disappointment.

You just don't know when, or where." Sally turns now and looks directly into Margaret's eyes: "Life disappoints. Doesn't it, Margaret?"

"All the time, Margie. All the time."

"Not even with any warn...." Sally is momentarily stunned. "*What* did you just say?"

"I don't know. What did I say?"

"You called me Margie."

"I did? Oh...I'm sorry. I didn't mean to."

"Margie was my older sister."

Margaret is near tears but fighting hard not to show them. "I'm sorry. I'm so sorry, Sally. I...uh..think I'd better be leaving."

The dogs are relentless. The garbage can topples, and the lid rolls off, drawing Sally's attention back to the window. "Oh My God!" Garbage is strewn everywhere, including a large brown paper bag which they begin sniffing and pawing at. "NO! NO! They mustn't!

She's gotten Margaret aroused. "Who mustn't!?!"

Sally runs out the back door of the kitchen into the alleyway between the cabins. "NO! STOP THEM! *Please*...STOP THEM!"

Margaret goes to the sink to turn off the water, watching Sally keeping her frightened distance from the dogs. They have partially torn apart a brown bag, revealing her soiled black dress, the dress she wore earlier. Tania, having heard the commotion, comes out of her cabin and calls off the dogs. They quickly cower away, leaving the remains of the bag with Sally's clothing on the ground.

Tania picks up the bag and the mostly visible dress. The bra and panties also visible are not addressed. Sally just stares at Tania in bewilderment and denial and asks, "Why is this in the garbage?" to disown the embarrassment of her involvement. Tania doesn't quite know what to say. Seeing Sally in obvious distress, though, she gently hands her the bag of clothes. In a sudden shift of persona, Sally regains full composure, having again repressed the events of the day. "This is so strange, though," she says in a rigidly normal tone. "Who could've done this?" Tania sees Margaret at the open kitchen window. They share a silent bewilderment. "And why?" asks Sally, "Why would anyone throw away such a pretty dress in the first place?" She's looking directly at Tania now, and then over to Margaret. "Can you imagine?" Tania looks at Margaret and Margaret back at her. Everybody's looking at someone.

Even Clarence, who's leaning against the passenger door, quietly observing at a distance, which is, after all, what Clarence does—always at a distance, always alone. One senses his compassion for Sally's plight. That he can perceive her incoherence, intuitively, almost clairvoyantly, without any explanation or factual account, is something he has within him. Just as Margaret, who feels something deeply familiar about Sally, calls her by her deceased sister's name, for reasons neither she nor we can understand, quite yet. Her making the trip to deliver Sally's few forgotten magazines is as much her effort to understand more, as it is concern about getting no answer when she phoned earlier.

"But weren't you wearing...." Tania is smart enough to back off.

"Oh well. I'll be happy to pay for the cleaning and any damage that's been done."

"Oh no no. That's okay, Tania. It's my fault, actually." Tania looks at Margaret, still at the kitchen window. She is shaking her head, no answer. "How's Bob?" Sally asks.

Tania, taken off guard, is flustered. "Bob? Oh – he's fine, thank you. I just spoke with him a little while ago. I understand Danny's taken to camp like a fish takes to water!"

"Yes. He's at the camp now, isn't he?"

Tania reassures Sally, "Yes. Yes, he is. They both are, actually." The campers are back in their bunks now, prepping for tomorrow and preparing to go to bed. "Well," says Tania, "I'll be seeing Bob shortly, if there's anything you'd like me to tell him."

"Is Danny coming home?" asks Sally.

"You know, that's a very good question. I *don't* know. Why don't I call Bob right now and find out?" Tania has her cell.

"Oh no, that's not necessary."

"Oh, I don't mind."

"No, no," Sally insists. "Don't. I don't mind if he sleeps over."

Tania checks her watch. "I'm sure they've already had dinner, though,"

"Please don't bother him. I'd just as soon have a quiet night by myself, anyway. I've got some good magazines that Margaret just brought over."

Tania, ready to dial, hesitates. "If you're sure?"

"I'm positive. Thank you, Tania. For everything." Sally looks over to her kitchen window where Margaret is standing, "Margaret, are you alright?" Margaret, speechless, just bobs up and down. "Well, I'll be fine, then," says Sally to Tania. Margaret comes out now to join them. "Thank you, both, so much. I'll be fine." Shockingly, Sally nonchalantly lifts the garbage can cover and gently puts her bag of clothes back in, carefully closing the lid, and as if in a trance walks quietly back to the cabin.

Tania and Margaret are speechless, standing silent and still, watching. "Strange, isn't it," whispers Margaret. "She's got her bags all packed and ready to leave."

"Huh? But she only just came up?"

"I know, I know, I told her that. I mean I said that."

Tania adds, "She's going through a very difficult time, Margaret. She's just lost her husband, you know."

Margaret's eyes widen, "Oh no. No, I didn't know that."

"Yes, it was Dr. Morris who'd suggested she use his cabin for a few weeks, just to get away."

"I had no idea," says a stunned Margaret. "How old a man was he?"

"I don't know actually."

"Well," Margaret concludes, "It's all so temporary, isn't it, dear? All I can say is thank god for the *now whats*."

"I'm sorry?" asks Tania.

"If it weren't for them, my dear, there'd be no damn reason to be here at all. You can't win. You–just–can't–win."

Clarence is at the wheel now. Margaret's the passenger. He's lost in solitary thought. "Well?" Margaret asks, "Are you going to sit there all night and dream, or are you taking me home?!" Ignition.

● ● ●

The cabin lights throughout the camp are off, the kids in bed. The night is clear, the stars are out, and the moon shines brightly, crickets chirping. Only Bob's cabin office is still dimly lit. He's closing things up now, standing against the file cabinet with an old sixties record player on top of it, holding the needle off the still-spinning disk with one hand and reaching for the record jacket with the other, just as Tania sneaks up from behind and thrusts both her hands into his front pockets. "What the...!" Though taken by surprise, he knows it's her—accidentally dropping the needle onto the spinning disk—REVEILLE! Holy Cow! Pandemonium! The cabin lights all come back on. Tania's pulling him away from the turntable. "What the hell are you doing!" The kids are raising hell and loving it! Tania's play-wrestling, pulling him back further still. "Are you crazy!" Once upon a time his camper, she's still the mischievous little girl.

The girls in Liza's cabin, in their nightwear or less, are having a time of it—pillows flying, total mayhem. Danny once again lifts himself up from under Liza's window. He looks for the same bed he first saw her standing in front of, but no she's not there—or anywhere else. The female counselor, meanwhile, enters the bunk to round them up, not noticing a pair of pretty sneakered legs under the toilet stall as the girls scurry back to their beds. "Okay! LET'S GO! Fun's over. If I don't see sixteen asses in bed by the time I count to five, you're all confined to the bunk tomorrow. One...Two...Three...

Meanwhile, Tania got what she came for.

• • •

"Psst...over here." Danny sees Liza in shadow under a tree. She's pointing Danny towards the woods. They both make a dash for it!

"Where the hell were you? I thought you fell asleep."

Holding her unlit flashlight Liza smiles, "You worry too much. I told you I'd meet you. I stuffed my bed in case of bed check. Pretty cool, huh?"

"Yeah. Cool," he agrees, as he leads them deeper into the woods.

"Where're we going?" asks Liza.

"Don't worry...follow me." He takes her flashlight. Having found his way into the camp this morning, Danny's pretty sure-footed about finding his way back. And pretty soon the tree arrow's pointing straight ahead—"Flaghole Road."

There's a stillness now at the Morris cabin area. The only light that's on is in Sally's upstairs bedroom. Her radio's playing "Blue Monday."

"WHAT'S THAT?" Liza asks out loud!!

Danny puts his hand over her mouth. "Sssh. She's still up. Be quiet."

As he removes his hand from her mouth she whispers, "I *like* that" (meaning the music). Stealthily, they approach the front door, the gravel crackling under their feet. Slowly, with his flashlight on and Liza behind him, Danny pushes open the door, hears the click of a shotgun cocking. The light of the flashlight hides their identity. A voice says, "Stop right there." They freeze.

Sally turns on the lamp next to her chair, her gun at the ready.

Stunned silence. "Mom!" Danny turns off his flashlight. Sally is examining Liza. "Whatsa matter, mommy?"

"Who's she?"

"This is, this is Liza. Why're you pointing the gun at me?"

Suddenly aware that she *is* pointing a cocked shotgun at her son, she quietly lowers the barrel to her lap. Three packed suitcases are by her side. "Why're you so late?"

"I didn't know I had to be home by any special time."

"Oh. You didn't, did you? Would you like me to sit here all night worrying about you?"

"I didn't know."

"Who's she?"

"My name's—"

"Liza's my friend, mommy."

"Your friend. I See. Have you been friends long?"

Danny lowers his head now. "No."

"I see. And where, may I ask, were you going?" Danny's head's still bowed. "Danny, I asked you a question." He shrugs. "How old are you, Liza?"

"Thirteen."

"That so. Well my young stud, you do like them young, don't you?"

"She's my age…we weren't going to do anything."

"You weren't, were you?" Danny, sheepish now and head bowed, just quickly nods no.

Changing gears now. "Well. Danny, your things are packed. We're leaving in the morning."

Danny is stunned. "Huh? Where're we going?"

"Away."

"But we are away."

Angered, Sally bursts out, "I'm not in the mood to argue with you, young man. We're leaving. Do you understand?!"

Suddenly, the bright headlights of an approaching car sweep across Sally's face. It slows to its gravelly stop. Sally reflexively turns off the lamp and whispers tersely, "Quiet. Both of you." Danny and Liza sneak quietly to the hallway stairs and peer through the railings between the landings.

Bob and Tania pull in front of their cabin. He douses his headlights and turns off the car. Tania, inebriated, is leaning on him. Hearing the radio upstairs, Bob bends over to glance up at Sally's lit bedroom. He's suddenly reminded. "Did you bring the kid home?"

Tania mumbles, "What kid?"

"Jesus!" Disgusted with her, he gets out of the car and approaches Sally's cabin. Except for the upstairs bedroom, everything's dark. He knocks gently on the wide-open door. No response. Once more he knocks. Bob gently calls, "Hello. Hello. Anyone home?" After a moment or two, he slowly enters, calling louder now, thinking she might be upstairs "Hello! Anyone home?!"

Suddenly Sally turns on the lamp. She's pointing the shotgun directly at him. He instinctively raises both hands. "Oh. Hi. Good evening. Beautiful evening, isn't it?

I'm sorry, I didn't mean to scare you, Sally. I…uh…I just saw the upstairs lights were on and the door was open and I just wanted to make sure Danny got home alright, that's all. I'm sorry if I frightened you."

"Yes, he did."

"Well. That's a relief! I frankly dropped the ball here. I wasn't sure if he wanted to sleep over or come home and, well, this is my fault really. I should've clarified this with you earlier. I'm sorry. He's still welcome to sleep over though, we've got an extra bunk, ya know."

"That won't be necessary."

"I see. Well, okay then, that's fine. 'S long as he's home safe and sound. I think he enjoyed himself today, though. He really got along well with the kids, that I can tell you. You've got quite a boy there."

It's as if Sally hasn't heard a word he's said. She's just looking him up and down the barrel of a gun.

"So...," Bob says with a nervous smile, his hands still raised. "Everything's okay then?"

"Everything's fine," says Sally. "Why shouldn't it be?"

"Oh. It should be. It *definitely* should be. And it is, actually. Actually, you're looking quite nice yourself this evening."

"What's that supposed to mean?"

"Huh. Well..uh..just..Just that. I mean, it's been...it's been a very stressful week for you, Sally. I...uh, I admire your strength."

"My strength."

"Yes. Your constitution. Dr. Morris filled me in a little bit and I... uh...I don't frankly know if a normal person could–I mean–not that you're not a normal person, My God–you're *super* normal—what I mean is given the *circumstances*, I'm not sure I could've held up as well as you have. Really. Sally? Would you mind lowering the rifle? Just a bit."

She does. Just a bit.

"Thank you."

"You think I'm crazy, don't you?"

"No. No I don't think you're crazy. Why would you say such a thing? My God, why would I think that? No. Absolutely not."

"Well I'm not, you know."

"Of course you're not. I know you're not."

"I've been through a very stressful time."

"I understand that, Sally."

"No, you don't. You say you do but you don't. How could you? I never should've come up here."

"I'm sorry...."

"She's probably told you everything."

"Everything? Who?"

"There's such a thing as shame, you know. That's probably something you don't understand, most men don't." There's a moment of silence. "Was it you?"

"Who me, what? I'm...I'm sorry. I don't understand, Sally."

Danny stares, troubled, through the stair railing. He's been listening to every word. Sally's suggestion of Tania triggers nightmares.

By now, Tania's gotten out of the car and approached the cabin. Given her wobbly condition, it's more of a stealthy meandering, but she's able to see Sally through a side window. She's literally stunned sober, her face against the window but out of Sally's line of sight. Bob sees her, though, and so does Danny.

"I'm really sorry," says Bob, "I'm really not sure what you're asking."

"I'm not sure. With a mask, you all look alike."

"I don't have a mask, Sally. Please, you're going to have to be a bit more specific. I really don't know what you're asking me."

"I don't think it was you."

"Would you mind pointing that away from me? It's very uncomfortable."

"Do you find me attractive?" Sally asks.

"Oh. Well. What to say? Now you've got me in a helluva spot. Damned if I do and damned if I don't. I think you're a very attractive woman, actually. Yes. I mean, I have to be honest. I hope you wouldn't hold that against me."

"More attractive than her?" Bob's face shows confusion. "Your girl-friend."

"Oh. Well. You're just very different. I mean, you're very different types."

"Am I your type?"

"Oh...uh...no.... I don't know, really. Honestly I haven't given this any thought, any thought at all, really. I mean, why would I? We've only just met, Sally, and briefly at that. It just...it just hasn't been a thought of mine – no slight to you, mind you. I hope you understand."

There's a moment of silence. Sally is tortured now by doubt. "I'm not sure. I'm just not sure."

Danny suddenly erupts. Tania's nose is up against the window. She ducks when she sees he's seen her. He just lets out with an open roar, his hand pointing at the window, "I don't trust her! She told him everything! She's a liar!"

Sally is looking now in the direction he's pointing—"WHO?! Who told him everything! WHO?!"

"She did! She told him. She's a liar!"

"*Who's* a liar?!" Who are you talking about? Danny Shut Up!"

"SHE'S A LIAR! SHE'S A GODDAMN LIAR! SHE'S A TROUBLE-MAKER!"

"SHUT UP I SAID! I SAID SHUT UP!"

"KILL HER!" he's screaming, pointing at the now empty window. "KILL HER!"

As Sally raises the rifle towards the far left window, Bob makes a dive for her. A shot goes off accidentally, hitting one of the rafters. Now on the floor, Sally is pitifully out of control, sobbing uncontrollably. She's fighting off Bob. "RAPE! RAPE! Tania comes running in as Bob hands her the rifle. "Oh God," Sally cries, "Oh God...God help me.... Help me...."

Bob gently cradles Sally in his arms while Tania places the call.

THE PARAMEDICS AND THE SHERIFF ARE THERE IN
no time, and you can be sure it doesn't hurt any that it's Dr. Morris' sister
who needs help. Even without a best seller, Joe Morris is a highly respected
member of this close-knit community, although, make no mistake about
it, celebrity has its rewards. Deputy Mackie carries Dr. Morris' paperback
in his back pocket. He's studying part-time for his MSW and was hoping
he might even get a chance to meet the good doctor, and perhaps angle an
autograph and, you know, a little chatter, and maybe strike up a relationship. It wouldn't hurt to have Dr. Morris's name as a reference someday.

Sally has calmed now as Bob gently leads her to one of the paramedics,
who assists her to the ambulance. She's hardly a delicate old lady. Sally's
one of those women, that *even* as an old lady, you'd imagine that she's
sturdy. As to her current emotional state, well, that's another matter altogether. Or not together.

"They're taking her away now," whispers Danny to Liza. They're both kneeling against the windowsill in Sally's bedroom, looking out from under the muslin curtains. "It's all his fault. I don't trust him. They're in it together. They just like to run other people's lives."

Mackie, meanwhile, has been taking notes on everything Bob's been telling him. Bob explains that Sally appeared to be perfectly normal when they first met earlier this morning, and then, this evening, she "just metamorphosed" into sudden derangement, became a different person entirely.

"Like two people?"

"Exactly," says Bob, "Two totally different people."

"What about the boy?" asks Mackie.

"Shy," says Bob. "Come to think of it, he's a lot like his mother. Not very trusting, almost paranoid you might say. I can understand it, though. I mean he's just lost his dad, for God's sake. But there's something else there; I'm just not sure I can put my finger on it. He was up at camp with us all day today, got along just great with the kids, everybody. He's even a bit of a skirt-chaser, but that's encouraging, far as I'm concerned. I'm sorry I can't give you more than that, officer."

"You've given me quite a bit, actually. Thanks." And with that Mackie reaches into his back pocket to put away his pad but realizes he's got something else back there. He takes it out and shows his copy to Bob. The book's a bit dog-eared. "He's your neighbor, isn't he?"

"You bet. Sally's his sister," says Bob.

"I know," says Mackie, "Chief filled me in. "I'd love to meet him though."

"Well, tell you what. I know he's on a book tour right now but next time he's up here, I'll make it a point to introduce you, how's that? You got a card?"

"Sure do." Mackie dips into his wallet and hands Bob his card, "I'd be really grateful if you could arrange for that, sir. I'm going for my MSW right now."

"Are you really? You're very good, you know. You'll make a terrific social worker. Whaddaya doing in a cop's outfit?"

"Well...gotta eat."

"Don't we all!" says Bob.

"Where's the kid now, do you know?" Mackie asks.

"He should be in the cabin. I'm not sure where anybody is anymore."

Mackie's partner, meanwhile, has been relaying all of this back to Chief Bowman at Headquarters.

Sally and the paramedic have entered the ambulance, with her sitting close to the door opposite him. A second paramedic, the driver, places the three pieces of luggage between them. Danny's been watching all of it. Tania suddenly comes running out, frantic, her cell in hand, the other reaching out to Bob. "One of the girl counselor's in trouble - a camper's missing." (Wonder who *that* could be?!)

Danny worries about what Tania's telling Bob now. They'd better leave. As the ambulance makes its slow departure, with Sally looking up now towards her bedroom window, Danny tears up. Barely audibly, he whispers, "Mommy, what did I do?"

• • •

Hidden in the shadows of the night, under the Dogwood trees, Margaret sits at the wheel of her car staring straight ahead through the windshield, her CB radio tuned to the police proceedings before her. She's got a front row seat at the ultimate reality show. As she knits, Clarence is feeding her the yarn from a ball of blood-red wool sitting in his lap, seemingly oblivious to the goings-on. The sound of clanking needles and her gum chewing syncopate the moment. "Surely a dress isn't worth shooting someone over. My God, even if the dogs *had* chewed it, which they didn't, *why* would she throw away such a lovely dress and then make it look like it wasn't even hers? It doesn't make sense."

"Don't look for sense," Clarence mumbles, cryptically.

"When I brought those magazines over, I knew something was wrong, I just knew it. I'm not surprised. I'm not a bit surprised. Makes no sense though."

"Don't have to make sense."

"You just never know what goes on in people's minds, do you?" Margaret looks over at Clarence. His stolid detachment is palpable. "You haven't heard a fucking word I've said!" Clarence, staring out the windshield, is still robotically feeding her wool. "Clarence! I'm <u>talking</u> to you!"

Clarence turns slowly towards her. It is a tight-lipped hateful glance. Two strangers staring at each. "You don't care, do you?"

Clarence shakes his head. Margaret looks front now, staring again out the windshield as much for self-protection from an implied challenge, as anything. "You know…if you had cared, it would have done us both a world of good."

Suddenly the ball of yarn lands in Margaret's lap, but she's unaware of it, lost in herself and her thoughts, staring straight-ahead. That phonograph record might just as well be playing under, back in time, now, reflecting in soliloquy…. "I've always accepted you, and wondered why…. *Why?* Who are you really? Who do you belong to, Clarence? Where am I in you, son? It's so tiring, such a charade. Why was this my fault? It *was* my fault, though, wasn't it?" Tears flow down Margaret's cheeks. "I wouldn't listen. Why couldn't I listen? Why couldn't I believe her? I don't know why. I want to believe her even still. I don't want to know any different. I want a part of her. I love her, still."

Margaret's eyeliner is dripping down her cheeks. Pagliacci. A tortured soul, she has borne her guilt, evoking sympathy in us. And as she turns towards Clarence, now, and sees him gone, she gently places her unfinished scarf on his empty seat. Her Maine Coon comforts her. Animals know.

• • •

Having seen Tania handing the cell to Bob now, Danny tells Liza, "She's telling him bad things again."

"Who is, Danny?"

Bob's on the phone with the camp counselor and Tania's with him. Danny sees Mackie making his way towards the cabin. "We haven't time," he tells Liza.

"She can't be missing," Bob's yelling into the phone. "How the hell do you lose a kid?!" Angry and frustrated, he hangs up.

"What happened?" Tania asks.

"Well you *know* what happened. One of the girls isn't in her bunk. Jesus, why me? I'm sorry, babe. I gotta get up there."

"Well, it's not *your* fault."

"What does it matter whose fault it is. I'm IT! This is crazy time. *You* almost got shot but I had the distinction of first in line. God knows what set her off. Like I told the cop, one moment she's a perfectly normal, friendly woman …and then – *whammo*! And her brother's a shrink if you can believe that."

"Well," says Tania, "maybe he should be shrinking his sister."

• • •

Mackie has entered the cabin. "Hey Dan! You around?" He's standing in the downstairs hallway and can hear the radio up in Sally's bedroom. He moves slowly towards the stairs. "Hey Danny. It's me. Dwayne. You there?" Slowly, he makes his way up the stairs and enters Sally's open door to the bedroom.

It's clear at first glance: The sheets are crumpled, the bed unmade. It's an unnatural ambiance of dishevelment, particularly for a grown woman, and, of course, the floor scrapes and the cell still lying on the floor near the end table. The scene speaks for itself. Careful not to disturb things for forensics, he takes his cell shots. Entering the bathroom, for no other purpose than to pee, he lifts the seat. "Well, well. What have we here?" Snap, Snap. Better pee elsewhere.

The night sky has suddenly darkened; there's thunder in the distance.

• • •

The rain's coming down pretty heavy now and its cold. Danny's holding the flashlight as the two of them make their way through the dense brush. He knows the paved road is up ahead but fog has settled in. "Where're we going?" asks a shivering Liza as they trudge their way through a thicket of dense brush. "I think maybe we'd better get back to the camp. They're going to see that I'm missing."

Danny just pulls her along. "Danny, you're not even listening to me!"

"I'm listening, I'm listening. This is the road back."

"Are you sure...?" Danny stops, confused. "We're going in a circle," says Liza.

"I found *you*, didn't I?"

Liza's reason is overridden by their shared passion. Maybe it doesn't matter where they're going.... "I guess so."

CHIEF CLAUDE BOWMAN, HIS FEET KICKED UP ON his wooden desk, holes in his soles, is talking with Mackie on a black Bakelite rotary telephone, circa 1950s. The phone itself speaks volumes. He's also got one of those large Rolodexes, pad and pencils, no computer in sight. He's a throwback to a simpler time – straightforward, affable enough, no bullshit and his southern heritage (Georgia) is right there in his voice. How he landed here's anybody's guess. Being from the land of Georgia peaches, though, Chief sure has an appreciation for the ladies. Even a little hint of one is enough to perk his lascivious streak and excite, voyeuristically speaking, what is probably his long-passive libido; "vicarious" would be the operative word. What we've got here now, with a pinch of police know-how, is the ticket to enticement. Chief's sure enticed.

"Mackie here, Chief."

"– Whatchyagot!"

"I think we got a crime scene here, Chief."

"What's makin' you think that?"

"I found some pretty hard evidence, Chief. Convinces me."

"Hard evidence, huh."

"Well let's put it this way. It couldn't be any harder."

"I just hope it ain't none of them psycho courses you been takin.'

What're we talkin' about?"

"Morris cabin."

"I know, I know Morris cabin – What about it?!"

"Looks like a struggle went on up here, Chief – bedroom floors are scraped, furniture's been moved around, bed's disheveled, rope tied to a bedpost, phone's on the floor. Like maybe she was tryin' to make a call."

"How do you know *that*?"

"I don't know it, Chief. I'm just surmising'"

"Well we ain't in the surmisin' business, Mackie."

Mackie takes the pause that refreshes. "Condom in the toilet?"

"You don't say. Whatever you do, don't flush it."

"No way. I peed in the shed."

"Well, maybe if he'd died with it on, and rigor mortis set in, we'd have something to hang something on. Sounds like the motherlode, though."

"You bein' funny, Chief."

"Goddamn it, Mackie. Get your head outta the toilet. Just leave it there. They took her to the hospital?"

"Yessir – just a few minutes ago."

"Well, seal it off then and I'll get with the collection team. Don't leave 'til they're there. Ya hear me?!"

"I hear ya, Chief."

"Check in with me to confirm...and Mackie?"

"Yeh, Chief."

"Did ya see what she looks like?"

"Pretty woman, Chief. Real pretty woman."

"That right. How old, you say?"

"Late 40s."

"That right?"

"Yes, sir."

"Where'd Bob Sherman go?'

"I'm not really sure to be honest, Chief. He gave me a pretty good interview, though."

"Uh-huh."

"Okay. Well stay on it 'til the team gets there."

• • •

Danny and Liza have made it to the edge of the main road. The traffic zooming by is sparse, and the fog so heavy that it's hard to see oncoming traffic. Danny's trying to wave down a lift with the flashlight whenever he sees approaching headlights, except that the vehicles are so shrouded in fog that they're practically on top of him before he spots them and vice-versa, and by then it's too dangerous for them to stop. Danny keeps telling Liza to step back from the road's edge. Meanwhile, they're freezing their asses off. Suddenly, out of the fog, a pair of chrome-studded head-lamps slowly emerges, revealing an elegant, highly polished Ford Model A Roadster. Guess whose?

It's as if the past, unfolding in the fog of night, has time-travelled into the present. The driver stops and rolls down his passenger side window as Danny approaches. It's Lyle, the delivery boy. He's almost unrecognizable in his formal tux, a Roaring 20s dandy – clean-shaven, coiffed, polite and well spoken. What still comes across, though, is that undercurrent of danger and, come to think of it, a loner quality, something he and Clarence share, except that Clarence embodies the sadness of an outcast and a depth of compassion and awareness that is absent from Lyle. They're sort of opposite faces of the same coin though, bookends on Margaret's shelf of collectibles. But it's cold. And it's raining.

"You kids must be cold. Where're you headed?"

"Uh…, back to camp." They really don't know where they're headed.

Lyle leans back and opens the door, "Hop in. I'll drop ya off. There's a fur wrap in back there that'll keep you warm. Warm and friendly," he says with a shit-eating grin.

It can't be more than three minutes into the drive before Lyle finally says something, having been staring at Liza through his rearview mirror, much the way he stared down Sally. Liza and Danny have both been uneasily conscious of it, squeezing each other's hand under the blanket. It's as physically intimate as they've been, except the circumstances are hardly ideal. "My name's Lyle, by the way. What's yours?"

She squeezes Danny's hand real tight now. "Liza."

"*Liza*. That's a very pretty name. Always liked that name. *Liza*. Real pretty. What're you guys doin' out in the rain like this?"

"We just got lost, that's all," says Danny.

"He your boyfriend?" Liza's squeezing *real* hard now.

"Yeah," says Danny, as if to say "you wanna make something of it?" "Yeah. I'm her boyfriend."

Lyle smiles and leans into his glove compartment. "I gotta girlfriend, too, ya know." Under a pair of leather gloves, he's fishing for and finds a black-and-white photo, passing it back to Danny, as Liza leans in.

"Whaddaya think?"

It's Margaret. She's wearing a white ball gown that's identical to the gown in the framed photographs on her bedroom walls. The shot was actually taken over Lyle's shoulder, probably not that long ago, while they were dancing.

Danny, unceremoniously, blurts out, "She's old!" Liza knees him.

"Well," says Lyle with a smile, "She sure as hell ain't *new*!" Lyle's again staring at Liza through his rearview, giving her the creeps. "Not nearly as new *and* pretty as Liza."

"*I* think she's pretty," says Liza, defending against any interest he might be harboring for her.

"Hey," says Lyle, as if he's suddenly had this unpremeditated brainstorm, "How'd you like to meet her?"

"I think I'd better be getting back to my bunk. I'm sure I'm in trouble. My counselor's probably already worried about me as it is."

"Sure, sure," says Lyle. "I just thought you'd like to go to the ball, that's all."

"There's a ball?" asks Danny. You mean like a *Cinderella* ball?"

Liza's *really* squeezing Danny's thigh under the blanket. He looks at her and she's nodding no. "We're not dressed for a ball," says Liza.

"Oh, that don't matter," says Lyle. "You can watch. Margaret *loves* it when people watch. You'd be surprised, though; She's a wonderful dancer. I'm not so bad, myself, to be honest."

Danny's looking affirmatively now at Liza, searching for her approval. But Liza's unsure. He's staring again at the picture with the softly blurred image of dancers dancing behind her, bringing alive, in his mind's eye, what increasingly *looks* like a ball. If only he could hear the music, if only in his mind, he could *believe* himself at a ball. It's as if the scene he's conjured has created their seat at The Ball, albeit less grand than imagined.

• • •

Clarence gently lowers the needle.

Margaret's expansive bedroom has been transformed, adorned like a ballroom, softly lit. The framed faux-Victorian ballroom photographs behind her are highlighted with pin spot lighting. The more Danny focuses and takes them in, the closer they seem to get, as if telescoped through a psychic lens, just like his lucid dreaming. What's lacking in 'reality' manifests through imagination. He and Liza are seated at a candlelit corner table with a white tablecloth, resplendent with soft drinks and cookies. Though bewildered, they're watching Lyle and Margaret dance an 1891 waltz. Danny had imagined a real ballroom, though, with dancers like the pictures on the walls. Clarence, meanwhile, standing in the shadowed corner opposite, keeps watch on their Victrola, and catalogue of one – "After the Ball." The lyrics are so haunting, though, that each time Clarence hears them, what might've been or could've been—while he may never know for certain—resonates still, with an undiminished knowingness.

• • •

Focused on the spot-lit photos on the far wall, Danny sees that the "ballroom" in these photographs is actually a college gymnasium. The banner strung across reads BROOKLYN COLLEGE GRADUATION BALL, 1980 Roaring 20s-style.

And as the dancers danced, the sad man sang...

"A little maiden climbed an old man's knee –
Begged for a story: 'Do Uncle, please!
Why are you single, why live alone?
Have you no babies, have you no home?'"

Margaret, dancing with Lyle, and lost in time, is drawn now to the picture just inches to her right.

A young man in the left foreground of the photo, his back to us now, appears to be checking his camera's ground glass, as the waiter fills his uplifted glass. In front of him, though, at the far end of the dance floor, is a couple. The mid-ground dancers, like flickering shutters, obscure his view. But he sees them clearly now, and if you knew *who* they were, you would too.

"I had a sweetheart. years, years ago.
Where she is now, pet, you will soon know.
List' to my story, I'll tell it all, I believed her
faithless, after the ball."

She moves now to the next photo. It's the same young man now, but photographed from the exact opposite side of the room, his camera still at chest level, and apparently at the *exact* same time, his glass still being filled. He looks aghast at what he sees! But why?

That Margaret could have been in two places at one time and taken *both* shots is impossible, quantum mechanics notwithstanding. Clearly, a Brooklyn College photographer colleague[**] would make more sense, the *only* sense. But whose shot is this? They can't *both* be hers, synchronicity notwithstanding.

And the sad man sang:

> *"Long years have past now, I never wed.*
> *True to my first love, though she is dead.*

· ·

[**] There is no mention of a student by the name of Margaret Meltzer in Brooklyn College's student enrollment records, covering the years of her possible attendance, either fully matriculated or part-time. This may yet be another of Margaret's confabulations in her quest for inclusion. How she ended up with these pictures on her wall is anybody's guess.

She tried to tell me, tried to explain—
I would not listen, pleadings were vain.
One day a letter came from the man;
he was her brother, the letter ran.
That's why I'm lonely, no home at all—
I broke her heart, pet, after the ball."

The fourth and final shot is of the young man again, and perhaps the other *is* her brother, or someone else or other.

Whoever took these pictures might not have known, the tale they cannot tell. So there it sits, atop her vanity, her prized possession, a Rollei... A witness with no mind.

Lyle's been dancing with Clarence now.

"After the ball is over, after the break of morn,...

And with interests elsewhere, Danny and Liza have quietly slithered their way down the hall towards the open storage room door, a room that faces the street.

...after the dancers' leaving, after the stars are gone,
Many a heart is aching, if you could read them all –
many the hopes that have vanished after the ball."

As the record runs out, Margaret turns now towards Lyle and Clarence. Lyle applauds her as Clarence goes to turn down the repetitive loping of a scratchy platter.

And Margaret, looking around at the empty room now...lost... whispering.

"Where'd it all go?

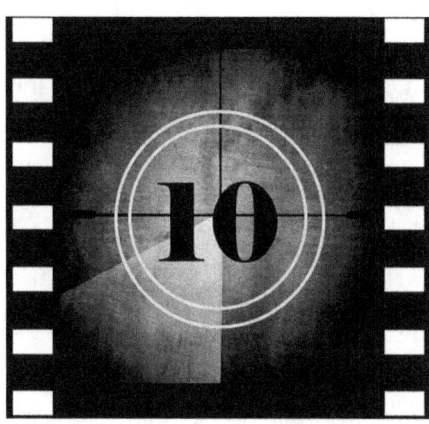

HEAVY RAIN IS PELTING THE STORAGE ROOM'S

moonlit window, as Danny and Liza embrace, the raindrops projected onto their bodies. There is the awkwardness of passion born of innocence, the underlying fear of sexual arousal. Danny nervously, anxiously, unbuttons Liza's blouse. "Danny. I'm afraid," she whispers.

"There's nothing to be afraid of. I promise, honest."

"Are you sure?" Danny is touching her nubile breasts under her partially unbuttoned blouse. "Oh, Danny. Danny, please be careful."

"I will...don't worry. I think I love you."

"Oh, Danny...I love you, too."

A barking dog. Danny's attention is suddenly drawn to the street below. The dog is drenched, begging to come in. Danny's passion for Liza incites a sudden guilt-ridden fear. A kaleidoscope of emotions. Their arrival at his uncle's cabin, the snarling Weimaraners encircling their car, Tania running out to stop them, his distrust of her sexual allure. Fear is in his eyes. This moment of pure, innocent passion is suddenly infused with the unresolved torment of guilt. Liza, unaware and consumed by her passion for Danny, has become an unwitting sexual aggressor. But she suddenly feels his distance.

As if from a dream-like distance, Liza's frightened voice filters into Danny's consciousness. *"Danny, Danny, what's wrong?!"* He responds as if himself in a trance. "She knows."

"Who does?" He does not answer. "Danny? *Who knows?*" Liza's fears are heightened. "Danny, what're you talking about?"

Suddenly, he breaks from Liza and she panics, *"Danny what's wrong!?"* He opens the storage room door and starts running. Liza cries after him. "Danny! *Danny! Where're you going?!!"*

At that moment, the store's delivery van comes gliding out from the side of the storefront, turning in the direction of the cabin area, and comes to a sputtering halt, the muddy tires smoking in the slippery traction. A gloved hand turns the ignition key, his foot pumps the gas, the back panel doors swing open.

Danny dashes to the back of the van and jumps in. Again he turns the ignition, this time it takes, pulling out of the muddy hole. Liza's onto the road just as Danny's closing in on the van's paneled doors. She's drenched, screaming through the pouring rain, "DANNY! DANNY! Wait for me!!" She runs frantically towards the truck, tires still screeching in the mud, picking up speed. Crying tearfully, Liza stops.

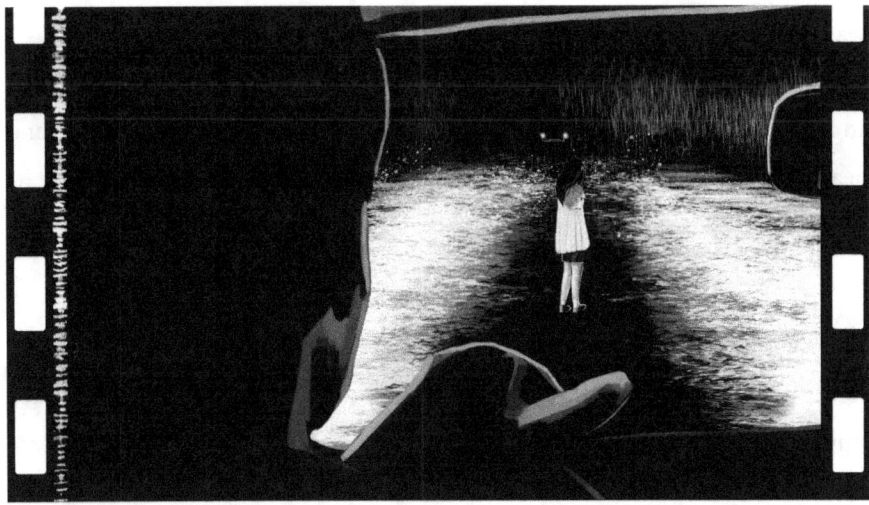

As she turns now to go back in, a pair of glaring headlights approach from the opposite direction. Liza, in the middle of the road, desperately waves her flashlight, hoping she'll flag it down. The car is flicking its brights, acknowledging her.

As Liza waits on the passenger side of the road, the car comes to a slow stop beside her and Bob winds down his window. "Where the hell have you been!? GET IN!" Liza gets into the car, and Bob reaches to the back seat and hands her a towel to dry herself off with. He's treating her as a father would a daughter, and the sense you feel is that he "gets it." He's angry, but he gets it. So does she. He backs up a bit, turns around, and heads back to the camp. Meanwhile, that poor dog, having scurried its way to the open porch door, has finally stopped barking.

● ● ●

Mackie's knocking on the Chief's door. Chief's on the phone, though, so he just motions Mackie in to sit. Mackie pulls Dr. Morris' paperback from his back pocket, putting it on the desk.

"Yes, doctor," says the Chief, "She's over there now. Last report I had they were taking her in for psychiatric evaluation. No, no, there don't seem to be no physical issues so far as I know. Yes sir, she's at Pocono General. I have that number if you need...oh, okay then. Oh." The Chief puts his hand over the mouthpiece and whispers to Mackie, "Where's the boy?" Mackie motions he doesn't know.

"We're looking for him right now, Doc," the Chief says into the old rotary phone. He's probably headed back to the camp. We've already got the neighbors on alert. Well, you know Margaret. Nobody gets lost around her 'less they're lost to begin with! This here's the best number to reach you at? Okay then, Doc. I'll call you soon as we got him safe and sound. Right." The Chief hangs up.

"Chief," says Mackie, "something went on up there, I just know it. A lot of dishevelment, the thing floatin' in the toilet...."

"I know all that, how many times ya gotta say it? You know for sure she came up here alone though."

"With her kid," says Mackie. "Just yesterday."

"I'll be damned. Course, we don't know the last time somebody flushed that toilet now, do we?"

Mackie adds, "Then there's this other stuff up there: pieces of black rope on the bedpost and floor, her cell down there too, furniture scuffs on the wood."

The Chief interrupts, "I know all that, damnit. You already told me."

Mackie takes out his cell now and shows Chief Bowman the shots he took. "We're missin' something, Chief."

"Yeh, we're missin' something – we're missing whoever the hell it is done this is what we're missing. You got the team on this, right?"

"Yessir," says Mackie. "They're up there right now."

Bowman reaches over for Mackie's paperback. "What the hell's this you reading?"

"It's Dr. Morris' book. I'm lookin' forward to meeting him."

"Well I'll be damned," says Chief, "Didn't know he'd gone and written a book."

"Yessir. Best seller."

"That right? I'll be damned. Hell, I was just on the phone to him a few moments ago. You heard me, you were standin' here."

"Yessir! You got me for a witness."

"We got a celebrity in our midst…," and regarding Mackie, "and an expert now in the makin'. I'll be damned."

• • •

The delivery van slowly approaches the cabins, headlights doused, engine silenced as it glides into the area and stops. Through the windshield the driver sees the glow of light from Tania's study and can even hear the tapping of her computer keys. His gloved hand on the steering wheel moves to remove the ignition key.

(But there's something else going on, isn't there?)

Meanwhile, about an eighth of a mile down the road, looking downwards with quiet embarrassment, sadness and relief, Liza sits quietly.

"You okay?" asks Bob. She shrugs demurely. "Well, we'll get you some dry clothes back at camp. You'll feel better." Liza senses he's not so much angry with her as he is genuinely concerned. "You wanna tell me about it?" She gives him a sort of *I dunno* shrug, a language all its own.

"Well, you don't have to if you don't want," says Bob. "I'm not as dumb as I look, though. I saw him running up ahead. Believe it or not, I was twelve myself once. Maybe more than once—I can't remember."

"I'm 13," says Liza.

"'Scuse *me* – I'm talkin' about him, though—is it Miss or Mrs?" Pure one-upmanship.

"Ms." says Liza.

"'Scuse me twice." He's looking at her. "Two for you," and ruffles her wet hair just to let her know that he's a good loser. He's got her smiling.

• • •

Having walked circuitously around the opposite side of Bob's cabin to avoid detection through Tania's open window, the driver's gloved hand reaches for the garbage can cover and removes the grocery bag that's still in there with Sally's clothes.

Danny, meanwhile, opens the downstairs drawer. Having never touched a live round before, the expression on his face is tentative, conflicted. He reaches for the rifle on the wall.

The driver, back at the van now, stops.

Danny's intentions are frighteningly clear.

Heading to Tania's cabin, the driver sees her light's on. It all feels so neat and syncopated, as if he'd planned it. Everything's going according to plan, with no plan. And here, two ships in the night…and never the twain shall meet. Yet.

At this instant, that flashlight is hovering from behind the muslin curtains in Sally's bedroom. The driver's antennae are drawn to two places at one time. One thing is certain, though. Danny's not upstairs.

Suddenly, Danny accidentally drops the rifle. Tania's dogs perk up, barking. Hearing them, and not far from her door now, he panics, picks up the rifle and runs to the far side of the cabin, concealing himself behind the brush. Tania, leaning out her window, sees the delivery van. The dogs follow as she goes to her front door. Clarence is at the van now, and the dogs affectionately greet their old friend. "Oh. Hi, Clarence. It's sort of late to be making deliveries, isn't it? Did Bob order anything?"

Clarence just shakes his head no. He's embarrassed that he's caused any trouble. "Well, I guess you've heard about Dr. Morris' sister?" Clarence nods his head yes.

"I wouldn't leave anything there if I were you. Bob's out now looking for the kids." Clarence shakes his head in understanding. She adds, "Okay, then. Stay dry. Goodnight."

Clarence waves goodnight.

One of the dogs has wandered to the other side of the cabin, the second one, about to follow. "*Hey*! – Where do you think you're going? C'mon! Both of you – I said get in here. Now!"

The other dog, having found Danny, is licking his face. Tania calls out, "Licorice! Where are you?!" Licorice comes around. "I said get in! NOW!" They're in, the door closes.

Clarence starts his ignition. Thinks better of it. Turns it off. A hand slowly drops the muslin curtain in Sally's bedroom.

Tania, meanwhile, is back at her computer, writing, the dogs at her feet. Again, they growl, low. "Now what's wrong?" They whimper. "C'mon. Both of you." She opens the basement door, ushering them in.

Cowering and whining they reluctantly enter and she closes the door behind them.

Clarence is looking up at the bedroom window. Dark. No flashlight. Danny, meanwhile, has reemerged, just entering Tania's cabin. The dogs are barking loudly. "SHUT UP!" yells Tania. The whimpering dogs can be heard behind the cellar door.

Bob, meanwhile, having delivered Liza back to camp, checks his watch as he heads back home with two large bags of take-out sitting next to him.

Danny, fearful of the dogs, is hesitant but he's already in the hallway, nearer the door, and starts to slowly move towards Tania's workroom. All is quiet except for the clickity-clack of Tania's computer keys. The dogs are whimpering, moaning in almost human tones, scratching at the door. Tania doesn't get why're they so disturbed tonight. She looks up from her keyboard and suddenly sees Danny's reflection on her computer screen.

Danny slowly raises his rifle and she sees its reflection coming in from the bottom of her screen. She's frozen still. "Danny?" She's beyond shock, speechless.

"You told him bad things about me?"

While disbelieving the surrealness of the moment, Tania's careful not to move a muscle.

"Danny? Who, Danny? Who've I been telling? What bad things? What're you saying?"

"It wasn't my fault. I didn't mean to do it. It just happened."

"Do what, Danny? What just happened?"

"You know."

"No. No, I don't, Danny. Honestly I don't."

"Why don't you believe me?" Danny asks.

"But I do believe you. Why *wouldn't* I believe you?"

"Where's my mother?" She hears his sudden tears. "I wanna see her."

She can see from his reflection on her screen now that he has lowered the rifle. "I'll take you to see her."

"You promise?"

"Can I turn around?"

Through his tears, "Yes."

Turning around very slowly and facing him, Tania says softly, "Yes. Yes, I promise."

The rifle drops to the floor now with a thud. Clarence, having been fearful of making any move that might've scared Danny, reveals himself from behind the wall. He gently picks up the rifle. Tania's stunned. "Clarence! What're you doing here?! I thought you'd left." The Clarence we experience here is not the Clarence we know. Though meek and soft-spoken, he is sympathetically reaching out. There is a profound sadness and sincerity that we're initially suspect of, given our lead up to this, but it is genuine, born of loneliness and a need for acceptance. This is as potentially familial a moment for Clarence as any he's experienced, and one he is attempting to contribute to, albeit not one he has planned. "I just wanted to make sure nobody got hurt is all. I was waiting 'cause I didn't know what to do. I didn't wanna scare him or cause no accident or anything. I'm sorry Miss Tania, I didn't mean to scare you either. I mean no harm. Everything's okay then."

Clarence probes down both chambers of the barrel with his fingers, as if to offer proof of Danny's innocence as well. "It ain't got no ammunition, Miss Tania. He had no bad intentions," and as he backs away, "I'm sorry if I scared you."

Danny whispers, "I wasn't gonna hurt her. I just wanted to scare her."

Clarence continues to slowly back away. "I'll leave now then."

Danny looks imploringly at Tania. "Are you really going to take me to her?"

Tania, deeply touched by Clarence, responds softly to Danny, "I promised you I would. As soon as Bob gets home we'll see who we need to speak with tomorrow to go visit her."

Bob's car is heard approaching in front. The dogs are it again, only this time one gets the sense of *their* relief at what they know to be their master's arrival. Tania stands up now, moves towards Danny, and musses his hair as he leans in trustingly towards her. She's hugging him close. Closure.

Clarence approaches the front door to leave, and Tania lets the scratching, whimpering, excited dogs out. They rush by her to greet their arriving master, running past Clarence. "Thank you again, Clarence," Tania calls after. He simply turns, looks at her, nods sadly and exits.

Bob, leaning into the car now and reaching for two large dinner bags, sees Clarence with the rifle. He's shocked and thinking the worst – "Clarence. My God!" but before he can utter another word Tania's at the door now, her arm around Danny, calling to Bob, "That's okay, honey. Clarence was very helpful. I'll explain later." The dogs are all over him now, jumping up and down and circling the wagon for food.

"Though relieved beyond words, he's still perplexed: "Clarence, what're you doing here?"

"Just trying to help things out, Mr. Bob."

That food's gotta be getting cold," calls Tania, "and we're hungry." She looks at Danny. "Right?" Danny nods agreement.

As if the tension of the moment never existed, the same as if Clarence never existed, Bob sees Danny under Tania's arm. "Well, whaddaya know! The mystery boy suddenly appears. 'Beam me up, Scotty!'" Even Danny manages a smile, and with the dogs still circling and jumping, smelling the food, Bob heads to the cabin. A family.

Clarence, an all-but-forgotten footnote, continues his lonely trek back to his van some several yards down the road. Tania, looking past Bob and seeing the lonely figure, knows somehow that he is headed back to nowhere. "Clarence!" she calls out. He stops and looks back now over his shoulder at the joyful group, understanding something he has never felt, his moist eyes betraying his depth of understanding, as with Margaret when she murmured, "Where's it all gone?" Tania asks gently, "Would you care to join us for some dinner?"

"We have plenty of food if you haven't already eaten." Stunned, pointing to himself as if for confirmation, he says, "Yes!"

"C'mon then," Bob says, "food's getting cold!"

Clarence's posture suddenly straightens, he walks back with a subtle lilt, a walk we haven't seen him walk before.

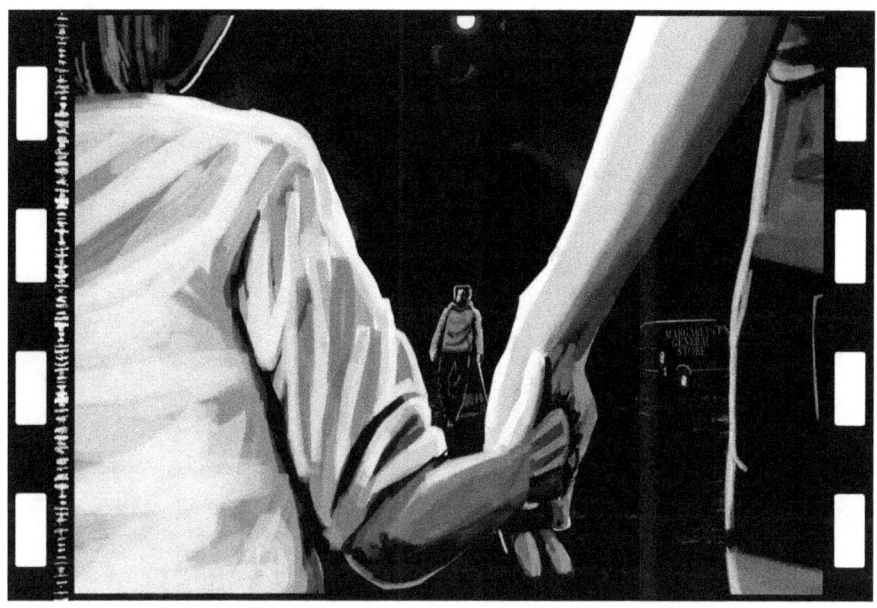

His value affirmed, Clarence has his place at the table.

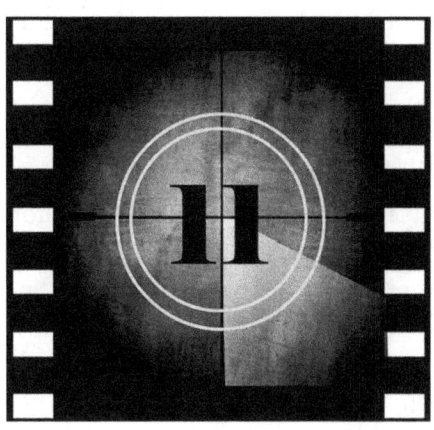

IT IS SAFE TO SAY THAT STROUDSBURG'S MAIN

Street, in today's Pennsylvania Pocono Mountains, will transport you back to a simpler, more innocent American way of life that was the 50s.

That Margaret would've somehow chosen to land here, given her generational Brooklyn roots, is understandable. Perhaps even more importantly, given her penchant for the preservation of the past, *her* past, and the seeming promise of a future that it held for her in so many ways—though unrealized, either botched or fated, Main Street is a reminder of that more promising time, still present in *her* mind, or at least a way station, holding things in stasis, with time to figure them out. This deep denial in which she has chosen to live her life offers the false comfort of a future yet to come that won't. Main Street is the perfect amnesia, a palliative, from the reality of a past that was. But for also a future that never happened and never will. So that's what got her here.

Clarence pulls the van in on Main Street first thing early next morning to get to the cleaners at 9 a.m. sharp. He has Sally's paper bag under his arm, the dress she'd thrown away that he'd recovered last night from the garbage in back. Talk about synchronicity. Can you imagine what might've happened had he *not* shown up, and the element of doubt he'd diffused simply by proving to Tania that Danny's intent with the gun and its empty chambers was fake? And what if his intent had not been so fake, god forbid. What if Danny had actually loaded the thing and Sally had been wounded and needed medical attention? The what-might-have-beens must not be so easily dismissed. Not to mention what he'd observed at the Morris cabin, thoughts of which still linger.

It's a chilly morning. While walking across Main Street on his way to the cleaners, he passes Cunningham's next door.

It's a busy hour for the breakfasters, mainly out-of-towners who enjoy good home cooking and not the hotel-style early morning buffets with their steam table medium-warm omelets, sugary buns and medium warm coffee from a packet of stuff in gray plastic carafes made with sink water. Nothing wrong with sink water—most of us use it—but there's something about hotel room sink water that is something less. Don't ask me why. Besides, ya gotta smell the beans, baby. The locals, too, enjoy the morning off, and fraternizing with the outside world is a bonus. Always a good time to spread the word about the good life, and Cunningham's is a throwback to the good ol' days. Long live the good ol' days.

The Dry Cleaner's window sign says "One-Hour Cleaning" so Clarence has an early start to get the job done and delivered.

He removes Sally's dress from the bag, splays it out on the counter, and asks for it to be cleaned and stitched where needed, examining and pointing to where the tears are as the clerk attaches safety pins, as needed.

A receipt generated, Clarence takes cash from his wallet and pays for the work in advance.

Meanwhile, a shrouded man in a sweater, having had his breakfast, exits Cunningham's.

That man, wearing a sporty gentleman's cap, is standing now at the cleaner's window, watching Clarence and the transaction that is occuring, as the clerk carefully puts Sally's dress into a cloth laundry bag. Feeling that odd sensation we've all felt at times, of being watched at from behind, Clarence suddenly catches the man's reflection in the mirror behind the counter, and instinctively spins around now to see who it might be. Shrouded under his cap, though, his head burrowed into his sweater, the man makes an abrupt turn and quickly walks off.

Clarence's instinct now is to turn and follow him but the cleaner reminds him that he's forgotten his change, and it's that brief turn one way and then the other that slows his exit. Looking now down the length of the street, the few out-of-towners and townsfolk roaming around on this brisk Saturday morning offer not a hint of a gentleman's sporty cap. What Clarence saw or might've seen, or thought he'd seen, who knows? It could've been the guy at the counter at Cunningham's having breakfast. The one wearing the sweater. And maybe having a sporty cap. But it could just as easily have not been. Clarence's face, however, betrayed a *knowingness*. He even felt the gentleman's stare *before* he saw him,[***] quite *coincidentally*, through the standing mirror behind the counter.

• • •

. . . .

[***] In *The Sense of Being Stared At,* author Rupert Sheldrake, PhD, writes, "If I look at someone from behind and he does not know that I am there, sometimes he turns and looks straight at me. Likewise, sometimes I suddenly turn around and find someone staring at me. Most people have had experiences like this. The sense of being stared at should not occur if attention is inside the head – but if attention stretches out and links us to what we are looking at, then our looking could affect the object of our attention."

Margaret's pissed. God knows why. But she's always pissed, so God probably doesn't care anymore, anyway. She's sitting at the register reading the local newspaper, including the events of last night, as Clarence enters. "Where the hell have *you* been!?"

"Out," he says, dismissively.

"Out?! What's *that* supposed to mean! You're not supposed to be out. *In's* where you're supposed to be. We got work to get done – just look at this mess!"

"You look at it." He disappears upstairs.

• • •

That afternoon, the receiving entrance of Pocono General Hospital has its typical 24/7 hospital ambiance. Dr. Frank, a psychiatrist dressed in suit and tie, approaches the nurse's station. He's a warm, slight man, not that that has anything to do with the nurse's station, though, but it might have something to do with the nurse. He asks for Sally's file and nurse Mary hands him her folder. "Thank you, Mary." He begins reading as he walks towards the elevators, then suddenly turns around, "Oh. By the way, Mary, we're expecting...." and the rest is drowned out by a loudish voice over the P.A. system paging one of the doctors. But apparently Mary got the gist of it (even though we didn't), except for the fact that he gives her his cell number and suggests, "Call me first, though," to which she playfully replies: "That's what you always say." "Now, now.." says the good Doctor, and enters the elevator.

Sally's in her hospital room, casually dressed and looking markedly better than she did last night. She's sitting in an easy chair sipping her coffee and reading a magazine. She appears perfectly normal, in fact – settled, rested and very much herself. There's a quiet knock on her door. "Come in."

Dr. Frank enters, gently, and sort of tentatively, less he be disturbing something, and in a very low-key way introduces himself, "Good morning, Sally. I'm Dr. Frank. I hope I'm not disturbing you."

"Oh, no. Not at all, doctor. Please. Please come in."

"I just thought I'd check in to see how you're feeling this morning."

"Oh, a whole lot better, thank you. Rested."

"Well you certainly look rested. I trust you slept okay?" He points to the empty chair opposite. "May I?"

"Oh please."

Dr. Frank sits opposite Sally and while her conversational tone is lucid throughout, an indefinable preoccupation or worry creeps in that he picks up on.

"It's probably the best night's sleep I've had in years. Whatever they put in that pill, I gotta get a bottle."

He's actually checking her folder, "Oh you mean...uh...benzo.... Let's see, what'd we give you here. Oh yes, I see—Dr. Kobilinsky prescribed Diazepam. Valium for short. Should ease any anxiety you might feel. I can write you a prescription for more if you'd like, you just have to be careful with this stuff, it can be habit-forming."

As they talk, he's writing the prescription and can't help but notice how she's wringing her hands. "I'll issue a one-time prescription you'll be able to pick up on your way out." As he leans forward and hands Sally the prescription, he asks, "Is there anything you'd like to talk about, Sally?"

"Oh no, thank you, Doctor. I just had a bad day yesterday. There's just been so much going on all at once. I suppose it was just a delayed reaction."

"Probably so. I understand completely." He shifts to a lighter gear. "By the way, I had a call from your brother last night and he explained some of it to me."

"Oh my God. I have to call Joe!"

"Oh, not to worry," calms Dr. Frank, "He actually called and asked me to check in on you and brought me up to speed after he'd spoken with Chief Bowman, our Police Chief. This is not D.C., ya know. We actually make decisions around here."

Dr. Frank is very good at establishing intimacy with his tone and friendly gab. He inspires trust on sight. "Ya know, Sally, anybody would have had a tough time holding it all together given what you've been through, especially having a young boy. I'd say you're doing a hell of a lot better than most of us would under similar circumstances. Anyway, in case you want to talk some more...." He hands Sally his card, "Here's where you can reach me. Just to give you a heads-up: With these kinds of things there's often a delayed reaction or setback. It's not unusual, but it's nothing to worry about, either. Besides, you're lucky to have brother Joe around – he alerted me as soon as he'd spoken with Chief Bowman."

"You're very kind, doctor. Thank you."

"Joe brought me up to speed on his way to Philly for his book tour. Your brother's a famous author now, ya know – who knew!" he says smiling.

"Well, I suppose that's true. Our father was a successful businessman who never thought his only…"

Dr. Frank's cell rings. "You'll excuse me." He answers. "Yes. Okay. Give me ten minutes. Thank you. Yes." He hangs up and back to Sally, "I'm sorry. You were saying?"

• • •

It's about one o'clock now and the hospital parking area is beginning to fill up. Strikingly, a red Tesla roadster pulls in and slithers into an open spot. Right behind is Margaret's delivery van, choosing a parking spot close to the hospital entrance.

• • •

"When my sister Jamie and I were growing up our father never thought Joe would ever amount to anything because all he'd ever talk about were his model cars. Us girls were his pride and joy," Sally says. "We frankly got better grades than he did, but please don't tell him I said that." Dr. Frank motions that his lips are sealed. "It's as if he used *us* as his way of expressing his disappointment and frustrations with Joe, saying things to him like, "Why can't you be more like your sisters?"

"That reminds me of a line from *My Fair Lady*," Dr. Frank interjects, "Where Professor Higgins sings, 'Why can't a woman be more like a man' except…," realizing, suddenly, he has nowhere to go with this, "—except here it's in reverse!"

"Oh," says Sally, not sure what the hell he's said. And after a brief silence for reflection, she adds: "Joe's not gay…. I don't *think*."

"Oh, no, no…," interjects the good doctor.

"Although it's true," Sally ruminates, "he's never been married."

"Oh no. I wasn't suggesting that—not at all! I have to be honest, though. My best friend Bob in high school always told me I came up with the world's worst analogies. He'd say something worldly, and then I'd try to top it with an analogy, only to find myself lost in the middle of it with nowhere to go. I'd even forget what he'd said that I was trying to top in the first place! Old habits die hard!"

Continuing with *her* train of thought, as if she hasn't heard Dr. Frank at all, Sally says, "They were never close, and there was a lot of resentment, on all sides. My father could be unrelenting in his criticism. Joe was captain of the basketball team. And when they'd lose a game, Dad'd blame it all on him. He was the captain, for crissake!"

"I understand," echoes Dr. Frank. "Sounds like he might even have been jealous of his own son. It's destructive in the extreme. Some kids go off the deep end when parental disapproval hits hard; I've seen it. Growing up, I had a friend who shot himself dead on account of it. Damn good-looking kid, too."

"I was always resentful of him," Sally continues.

"Of Joe?"

"No, no. Our father. I think all three of us girls were, that he'd hold us up as a weapon against our own brother. I guess being an only son, who couldn't give a shit about our father's real estate business, Dad saw it as some kind of betrayal."

"Sounds like your father coulda used a good shrink!"

"We *hated* the man. All of us did. Joe included."

"I'm sorry," says a muted Dr. Frank.

Sally, having released pent-up anger, and the sudden sense of relief brought on by it, smiles. "Maybe I should take another benzene."

"Huh? Oh no, no – you don't wanna do *that*. It's good to clean paint brushes with, but it's carcinogenic! You, you mean Diazepam...*Valium*. I think you're thinking of Benzedrine. Kinda famous back in the 50s, the Beat Generation. But that wouldn't be a good idea, either."

"Oh, that's okay. I feel better just talking! You're very good, ya know – you really are."

"Well," says a stunned Dr. Frank, "thanks. I try."

"Maybe the world needs more Dr. Franks!" adds Sally.

Not immune to flattery, he muses, "Well, ya know, I've always said anger can be a very powerful fuel when channeled in a positive way. I'm not sure too many of my peers would agree with me, though, but brother Joe didn't turn out too bad, did he? If it works, don't fix it.'"

Touché!" seconds Sally with a high-five. "And now all Danny talks about are his model cars. He obviously got that from Joe. But I've been very careful not to fall into that trap with him. I've always encouraged him to go for it! whatever "it" was. If he turns out to be a famous racecar driver, or even a car mechanic, so long as he's happy, that's all that matters. But I hope he's a famous racecar driver," Sally says, laughing.

"Well," adds the good doctor, "he apparently admires his uncle. Who knows, maybe he'll end up another Mario Andretti. You know what *he* said: 'If everything seems under control, you're just not going fast enough.' For better or worse, some things in life we just don't know. Or control."

"That's true," Sally acknowledges with a smile, "adversity has a way of evening things up, doesn't it? Getting even."

There's a sudden knock at the door. Dr. Frank checks his watch and stands up with a broad smile on his face.

"Now I've got a surprise for you…if you're up for surprises?" He approaches the door.

"Just so long as they don't sneak up on me *after* you've opened it!"

He's momentarily startled. Dr. Frank can't help but pick up on Sally's comment. He knows more than he's revealed, including what he's already gotten from the police report and forensics. But it's literally only a split-second pause. Smiling, he opens the door and calls, "Come in!"

"*Mommy*!" Danny enters and runs to his mother's open arms. Tania and Bob remain standing at the door. "Mommy, can we stay?"

Sally isn't quite sure how to answer him but she's feeling awfully good, just doesn't want to lie to him. "I'm not sure, honey." "Well," says Bob, "Danny's welcome to stay with us at camp if he'd like. I know we've got an open bed in one of the bunks."

"Well," Sally says, holding Danny close, "would you like that?"

"YES!"

"I suppose then...." She looks to Bob now. "If you're sure this isn't an inconvenience."

"Not at all," says Bob. "He's already one of our heroes! Right, Dan?"

Danny nods in agreement and Sally adds, "I'll be happy to make the financial arrangements for his stay..."

"Not necessary; already taken care of," says Bob with a smile.

• • •

Clarence enters the lobby of the hospital. Dressed in his best: slacks and a jacket – a new man, with a sense of self-esteem we've not seen before.

Like Clark Kent, he had to have changed in a phone booth, but there are no phone booths, so probably the van. He wears his newly purchased Greek-style fisherman's cap like a true sportsman. He might've gotten the idea from that guy at the window, who knows, but this one's a lot more stylish. With the dry cleaner's box and a greeting card under one arm, and a bouquet of roses on the other, he approaches Mary at the nurse's station. She's just as stunned.

"Clarence? Well look at you, will ya. I almost didn't recognize you. What can I help you with today?"

Clarence fights his inherent shyness. "Hello, Nurse Mary. These are for Miss Sally Morris. I'm sorry, I don't know the room number…."

"Well, that's okay. I can have them brought up to her if you'd like." Checking the clock on the wall now, she says, "Visiting hours are almost over now but you can always come back at 4 if you'd like to do it yourself. She's with her son now anyway, and there are some other visitors up there, as well."

Clarence's eyes are downcast in disappointment, even though he never even allowed himself the thought of seeing her in the first place. That somehow would not have been right anyway; it would have appeared as if he wanted something in return.

"I see," says Clarence, "I will leave these with you then, if it's okay." He gently places the roses and the dry cleaning, with the card on top, on the nurse's counter.

"You sure you wouldn't like to come back later?"

Clarence doesn't so much respond as slowly back away, holding his cap in front of him. "I don't wanna bother nobody."

"I'm sure she'd be happy to..."

"Is she okay now?" Clarence asks.

Feeling his discomfort, Mary assures him, "Oh yes. Yes. She's fine. These roses are gorgeous, Clarence. I wish somebody would buy me roses. I'm sure she's going to love them. I'll make sure to tell her these came from you and that she gets it all."

"My card, too...."

"Yep. Your card, too."

"Well - that's enough then." He continues backing away and gently tips his cap. "Thank you, Nurse Mary."

At just this very moment, Dr. Joe Morris enters.

He's got his black satchel briefcase and a shoebox-size gift-wrapped present for Danny. He approaches the nurse's station just as Clarence is backing away, facing Mary. "Well, Hello, Mary. How've you been?"

"Dr. Morris! We haven't seen you in a *long* while. How've *you* been?"

"Busier than ever, I suppose. Sometimes I think too busy. Not that I'm complaining, though. I'm supposed to be on a book tour. I should be in Philly right now, in fact. I think I may have gotten three hours of sleep in the last two days."

Joe turns and notices Clarence, but not without a double take. He sees the flowers sitting on the counter. "Well, well, now – what have we here?"

"Clarence was just leaving these for Sally."

Dr. Morris turns to Clarence. "Clarence! How've you been, my boy? You know, I almost didn't recognize you." Joe picks up the roses and takes a smell – "These roses are gorgeous! This is very sweet of you, Clarence." Dr. Morris reaches into his jacket for his wallet. "What do we owe you for these?"

Profoundly hurt, Clarence is speechless. He shakes his head. "Oh no..., no. This is from me," he implores. Clarence backs off just to distance himself from any compensation."

"Oh no, Dr. Morris," echoes Mary, "Clarence was just...." "This is from *me*," Clarence confirms. Exactly what he'd feared – that he would be misunderstood as wanting something. After all, why else would he do it? "It's from *me*," he implores of Dr. Morris - "I don't want noth—"

Morris cuts him off. "Well, I'm sure Sally will be quite touched and appreciative, Clarence. I'll make sure she gets these. Thank you."

"But please tell her this is *my* gift. This is from *me*. She is my...."

Dr. Morris suddenly turns and looks Clarence fiercely in the eye, foreclosing any further discussion. "She's your what, Clarence?"

There is visible anguish on Clarence's face. "Aunt. She is my *aunt*."

Dr. Morris, totally dismissive of this absurdity, glances over at Mary now and winks at her. "Yes, of course she is."

"And you are—"

Morris spins back around and cuts him off. "Yes, that's right, Clarence. I'm Dr. Morris. And I am very tired. Now that'll be all, thank you, and I'll be sure she gets these." Dr. Morris gathers the roses and puts the dry cleaning into his satchel.

"That's okay, Mary. I'll take these up to her. Is Dr. Frank up there yet, do you know?"

Though shaken, Mary responds professionally. "Yes, doctor, I believe he is and so are the camp people—I forget the camp owner's name."

"Oh, you mean Bob Sherman, my neighbor. Good man, Bob. Is Tania with him, do you know?

"I believe she is, yes sir. They're in room 425, doctor."

"425. Perfect. Thank you, Mary." Joe Morris takes a kind of gruff possession of the roses and the dry cleaning. It's as if Clarence is no longer there.

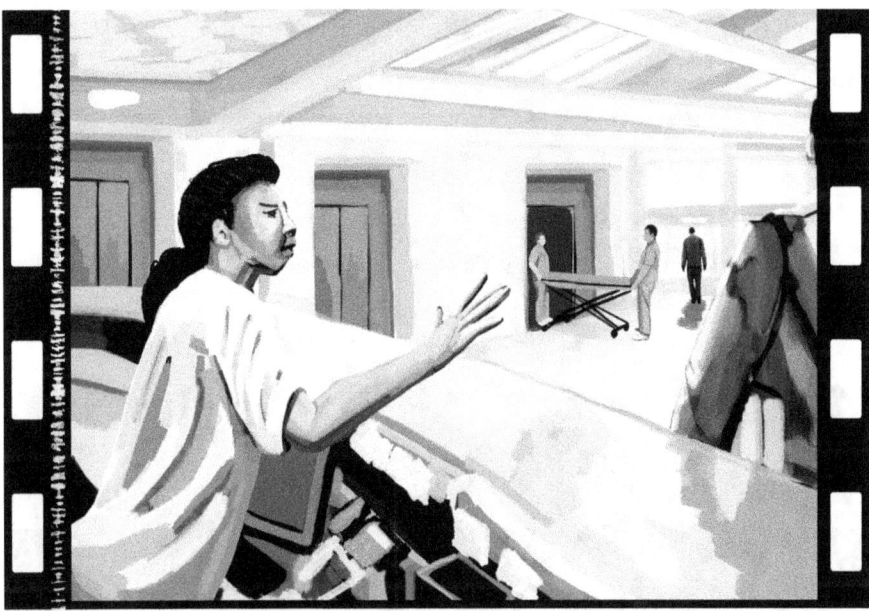

Mary watches Dr. Morris walk away, not understanding his insensitivity, even if Clarence is delusional. What harm did he do? Even if what he was saying is nonsense, he was only trying to express, perhaps, a need to belong and what is clearly from his heart. That is at the very soul of this community. Others, in fact, including Chief Bowman, have sent flowers.

Clarence, by now, has reached the entrance. "Bye, Clarence," Mary calls. "Don't forget to visit us again soon, okay?" And while her touch is subtle, she has lessened Dr. Morris' curtness.

Clarence is walking now towards the van. Deflated, lost, and in search of his own unanchored identity, he is perpetually reinforced by returning to a past he never lived, and an unlived present that's been stolen. His walk and body language are of a young man grown old. And Margaret, having mistakenly pre-judged and foreclosed the possible, has enabled a perpetual reinforcement re-living of the past, at the expense of a future. Two people bound as one. Mirror images of the same coin.

Dr. Morris, meanwhile, is in the hospital elevator as the doors close and it ascends. He opens Clarence's card to Sally and begins reading. The handwriting is printed in pencil, as if by a man many years Clarence's junior.

Dear Miss Sally,

I hope you are feeling better.

I thought you would like to have this.

I had it fixd and cleaned.

You are a very kind lady.

And you have a very good boy.

you friend, Clarence.

(the stock boy at the store)

He folds it in half…

….and rips it up.

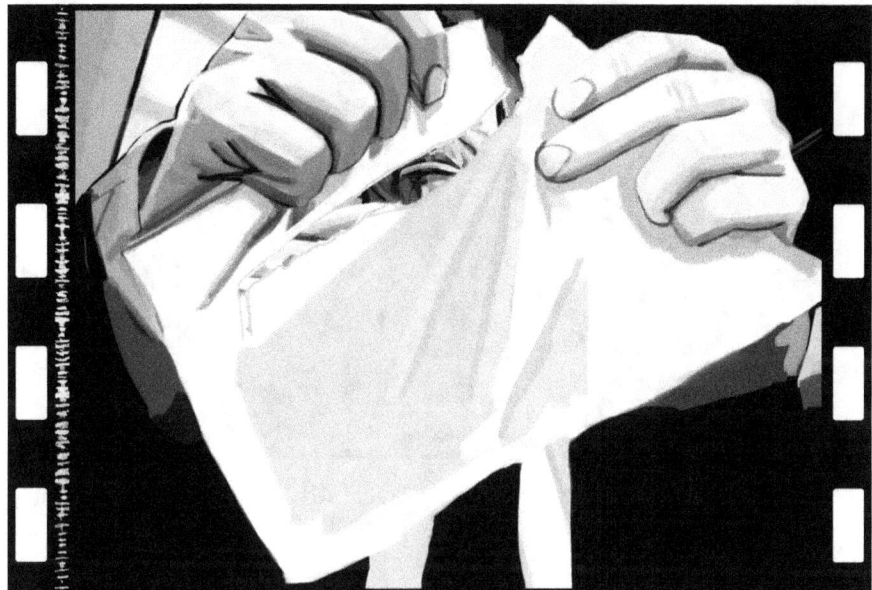

At that very instant, a gunshot rings out from somewhere outside the elevator. The few doctors and nurses in the elevator turn to each other, stunned. As the door opens on the third floor, nurses and doctors are seen rushing to the windows facing the parking lot and there are calls of, *"Someone's been shot!"*

He'd kept one for himself, resting peacefully now in his lap, but he'd made certain Sally had a full dozen.

• • •

"THEY'RE LOVELY, JOE. THEY'RE ABSOLUTELY LOVELY,"
Sally says as she arranges them in a vase.

The gang's all here and Danny's on the bed playing with his newest acquisition – a red Tesla Roadster. "You like that, huh? I got a surprise for you," says Uncle Joe. "You up for surprises?"

Danny nods his head, enthusiastically. Joe looks at Sally. "You mind if I take him fishing?" Then, confirming with Danny, "You still like to fish, right?" Again, a whopping confirmation.

Sally hesitates, but just for a moment or two, not longer, a sudden frown on her brow. She's wringing her hands just as she did when Dr. Frank noticed it then as he's noticing it now. "Well sure," Sally says. "I don't see why not." And then she adds — "But no excuses about the one that got away!" Sally's even got her sense of humor back.

At this point Dr. Joe stands up in what has become a very crowded gathering, and thanks everyone. First, there's Dr. Frank. Dr. *George* Frank who, as it turns out, is an old college buddy of Joe's (Dr. Frank never did mention that, did he?). And then Bob and Tania.

"Bob, is it okay if I bring him back to the camp by six?" asks Dr. Joe.

"That'll be perfect. See you guys at the mess hall — Why not join us, Joe?"

"Well, if I haven't collapsed from sleep deprivation and assuming you have an extra seat at the table?"

"You bet!" says Bob. And Danny's got a Teddy Roosevelt "De-light-ed!" smile on his face.

"Might even have a few fish in the offering," adds Joe.

"Well," says Bob, looking directly at Danny now, "Catch a big one, Dan. Then we'll have Nathan cook'em up!" And then, "Oh. Hey," says Bob to Danny, "I almost forgot...."

Bob addresses Sally and Joe. "Mind if I borrow him for just a minute? Man-to-man stuff."

Bob opens the door and leads Danny into the Hallway. He pulls a small envelope out of his shirt pocket. "Liza asked me to give this to you. She asked if you were staying and I told her I really didn't know." Danny opens the letter. There's a neatly folded note inside, and Danny kinda smells it before opening; Smells familiar. He rapidly but carefully opens the note.

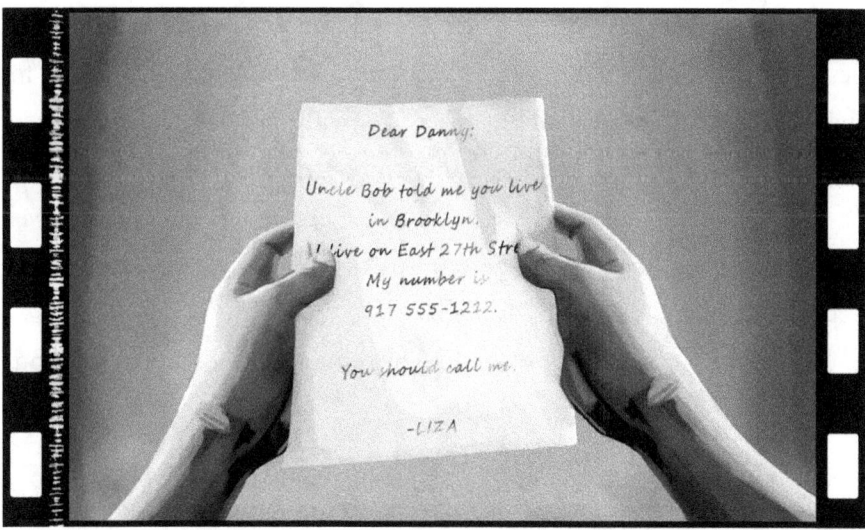

Dear Danny:

Uncle Bob told me you live in Brooklyn.

I live on East 27th Street.

My number is

917-555-1212.

You should call me.

– LIZA

"*WOW*! She lives on East Twenty-seventh Street. Did you tell her I'm on Twenty-ninth?"

"Well, I figured you'd tell her that," Bob responds.

"Cool. We're only two blocks away; I could ride my bike over."

"You better put that away. Just to keep it between us."

Danny folds it neatly and puts it into his pants pocket. "Yeah, Mom's liable to get jealous."

"Well, let's not go *that* far. All set?"

Danny and Bob re-enter Sally's room. Bob says his goodbyes to Sally, Dr. Frank and Dr. Joe. Sally offers her profuse appreciation to Dr. Frank for all that he's done for her. There's also a bit of unfinished business on her mind, though, and she expresses her apologies to Bob for the way she behaved last night, that it's really not her, and how sorry she is for having put him and Tania through all of this. Bob couldn't be nicer about it, assuring her not only of his understanding but even his appreciation for having gotten to know her and Joe that much better, and what a great kid Danny is.

"I wouldn't mind having one like him myself," adds Bob, for Danny to hear, as well.

"Not too late," smiles Dr. Joe!

Tania just lowers her head like she didn't hear it and is first out the door.

Everyone's feeling great except, perhaps, for the lingering elephant in the room that nobody notices. Well, maybe not nobody. As Bob and Tania leave, Dr. Joe asks Tania, "How's your book coming along?"

"Slowly," she responds.

"Tell me about it. Stick with it. Remember, 'Inch by inch it's a cinch; yard by yard it's hard.' And as my Pulitzer Prize-winning author friend, William A. Henry III, used to say: 'All writing's re-writing.' And he knew—two Pulitzers before he was thirty. Not too shabby."

Dr. Frank chimes in gently, "You know where to reach me, Sally."

"Yes, thank you doctor."

• • •

So now it's just the three of them. "How'ya feeling?" Joe asks Sally.

"I could use a vacation."

"Mommy, I thought we were *on* a vacation."

"You and me both," adds Joe.

Looking at his watch now, Joe reminds Sally that their sister, Jamie, should be arriving any minute now. Since Jamie's husband Max is away on a two-week business trip, Joe points out that it's really perfect timing, particularly since the two of them haven't seen each other in more than a year.

Sally muses, "Has it really been that long? I can't remember *not* seeing her, if that makes any sense."

"Makes all the sense in the world," Joe points out "the way you guys *tap, tap, tap* on your phones all day, you *think* you've seen her. Pretty soon, nobody'll talk to anybody and I'll be outta work!"

"You know, I never thought of that. You may be right."

"I'm not worried. With their virtual reality goggles they'll be at my office in no time, literally, and forget they never left home! Great convenience. Irony is, they'll be calling 'cause they're lonely. On the other hand it might be good for Weight Watchers. You wanna pig-out? Put on your VR goggles and try a fine restaurant, eat your heart out. Power of suggestion. Mind over matter. You'll be all filled up in no time. And think of the dough you'll save on cab fare."

"Well," Sally reasons, "If you're sitting there with a knife and fork... and *believe* you're eating, I guess you're right, especially if you already know what it's supposed to taste like."

"Seeing is believing, no question," says Joe. "Worse case, it'll be like a Chinese dinner. Take off the goggles and you're hungry again."

"Did you just think this up?" asks Sally.

"No. *You* did - *you* can't remember *not* seeing Jamie. *Tap, tap, tap.* Before you know it, nobody – literally, *no body* – will know the difference. Everybody's gonna be lonely but nobody's gonna know why. That's where I come in."

IT'S APPROACHING SUNDOWN ON FLAGHOLE ROAD
now, quiet, peaceful this time of day: cricket time. Deputy Mackie's
patrol car glides to a slow stop over the gravel, just in front of the Morris cabin. He gets out of his vehicle and heads to the front door, which
is taped but not locked, technically still potentially a crime scene. He's
still a lone wolf in this matter but something's grabbed him and he
can't let go. Makings of a great cop, right there. He heads up the stairs
towards the bedroom. The door is taped, but Mackie can't help but
notice that the police tape's been tampered with. He hesitates and
takes a cell shot. Putting on a pair of surgical gloves so as not to con-
taminate what the team may still be looking at, he meticulously
searches every crevice of the bedroom with his flashlight for potential
missed clues. Suddenly he sees a key wedged at the foot of the bed-
frame in-between the mattress and box spring. He carefully lifts the key
from the wedge.

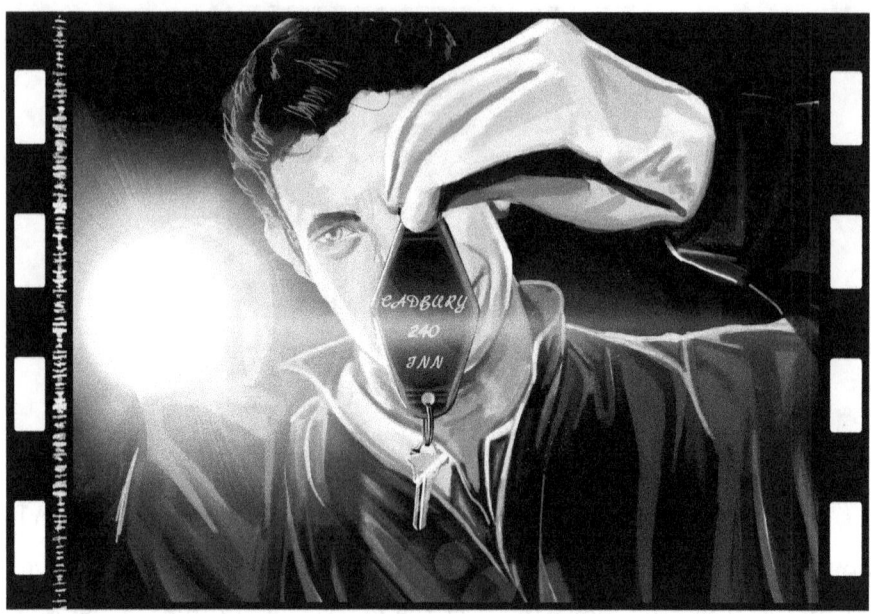

There's a tag attached to it: "Cadsbury Inn – #240." The small Town of Cadsbury is one town over—a 20-minute drive.

As Mackie approaches the Town of Cadsbury, he can't help but notice the welcome sign on his right: WELCOME TO CADSBURY, Life Like It Used To Be Pop. 2,341. And just about 100 yards up ahead on the right is the lit VACANCY sign for the Cadsbury Inn, only a few cars parked in front. Mackie pulls in and turns off his motor. He does take a moment, however, to take a read on the car license plates and notates them. The inn manager's curiosity is understandably piqued, and he comes out the door of his small Manager's Office/Reception Desk Entrance. "Evening, Officer. I'm Bert, manager here. Anything I can help you with?"

"Hey, how ya doin'. I'm from over Flaghole. Ya gotta minute to talk?"

"Sure. Sure thing, officer."

Inside, the manager goes behind his counter and Mackie stands opposite. "I'm doin' a little investigatin' an' I was just wondering if I can take a peek at Room 240."

The manager turns to the mailboxes behind him, rubs his hand along the box for Room 240's key. "Uh... I think 240 may be occupied, officer. No key. Yessir, they must be out. Is something wrong, officer?"

"Any idea how long they been checked in?"

"Well...uh...lemme see here." He moves over to his computer terminal against the sidewall to the left of the desk but otherwise out of sight. "I think they been checked in since...this morning, actually. Yes, of course. Nice young couple. About 8 a.m. this morning. I ain't got no Bonnie and Clyde here now, have I?"

Bert is an open-faced, affable family man in his 50s. He's one of those born worriers and if he's worried about anything, anything at all, you'll know it because it'll show right there on his face.

Mackie asks, "Any idea who was in the night before?"

"Night before, night before, well lemme see."

Bert heads back to his computer terminal. The screen shows that the room has been vacant for several nights.

"Lemme see now. Night before...looks like we were having an outage. That's right, our computer went down."

"Uh-huh. An outage. You mean you lost power."

Bert explains, "Well, uh, no. Not exactly. We had electricity if that's what ya asking. Computer issues. Woulda hadda been a paper entry."

"I see," says Mackie. "You got them paper entries?"

Now Bert's getting flustered. "Well, let's see now. What night was that?"

"Last night."

"That's right. Last night." Bert ducks down now, rummaging through a cigar box under his desk. He's actually got a couple of cigar boxes under his desk. "Last night. Right."

Mackie's looking on, hearing the rustling of papers, and sensing Bert's nervousness, but he stays nonchalant about it all. "And if you can check the night before that, too, I'd be appreciative."

Bert repeats, "Night before that, too. Yessir." More sounds of papers rustling.

Mackie gives it a beat. "Whatever else ya got down there under Outages."

"Outages. Right." Bert's shuffling now with *both* hands, from one cigar box to the next, back and forth. Sounds real busy down there. Almost like a tossed pasta salad, al dente. He's increasingly nervous, though. You have to wonder why.

While Bert's down there rummaging, Mackie gets the picture and asks, matter-of-factly, "By the way, Bert, anybody lose a key that you know of?"

Bert pops back up. Dwayne pulls the key from his shirt pocket. "Huh? Oh!" says Bert, and checks out the key. "I'll be. This is the key alright. Yep. 240. Just like it says." Either instinctively or make-believe instinctively, Bert goes back to his computer screen. All he sees is the word 'vacancy.' It's all coming back to him now. "That's right. That's right! He lost his key. He kept askin' if I was sure he didn't give it back to me and I kept tellin' him not to worry 'bout it 'cause we weren't gonna charge him for it or nothin' like that. And I made another key that I gave to the young couple this morning."

Bert again checks the computer but his screen hasn't changed its mind. "Nope. No record." Dwayne stays kind of quiet just waiting for the other shoe to drop, and he knows it will, because for whatever the reason, Bert's not telling the whole story, though he's still talking. "He paid one night in advance, though. Didn't even have to ask for it. Now that I remember."

"Good thing you had an outage," says Dwayne, "Or you might not have even had a customer."

"Well I guess that's true. That's true. Guess, so...."

"Why so?" says Dwayne.

"Well...like...uh.... But come to think of it, he did say he preferred to pay cash anyway. What I mean is, he asked if he could pay cash. I couldn't've run the card check without the computer anyway, so I figure it's still legal tender as far as I know."

"Uh-huh."

"Even gave me a tip, if you could believe it."

"Oh, I'd believe it. Whadaya say your name was?"

"My name? Bert. My name's Bert."

Dwayne extends a friendly hand, "Dwayne. Nice to meet ya."

"Yep. Twenty bucks. On the barrelhead."

"Damn. You lucky dog, you." Now he does a tad more baiting, "Bet it got even better than that, huh."

"Huh?"

Dwayne just winks.

"Oh. No. No. Now, now, wait a minute, officer. It's not what you're thinkin'. Nothing like that. I didn't do nothing wrong or anything like that if that's what you're asking."

"Oh, no, no, Bert. I'm not ask—"

Bert is open, genuinely vulnerable. "I'm a family man. Two kids. My wife ain't been well lately. I can't afford to get into any kinda trou—"

"Bert, Bert. Trust me. I understand. I ain't lookin' to get you into trouble. Been there myself, my friend. Sorry to hear about your wife, though."

"I mean, trying to make ends meet on what I make here, officer, it's hard enough."

"Bert. My friend. Listen, ya gotta trust me." Mackie's looking up at the Security Camera on the ceiling behind the desk, facing him. He's checking out the corners of the other walls, as well. Mackie points to the camera above Bert. "By the way Bert, are we on the *out*age up there or the *in*age?

"Huh?" Bert looks up to check it out for himself and sees the small lit red light. "We're on the *in*age."

Mackie asks, with a little wink, "Ya think we can, ya know, outage it?"

A slow smile crosses Bert's face. His body language eases up, too. "Are you shittin' me?" Bert looks at Mackie with 100% open-faced trust, grinning broadly, and with a sense of relief and confidence that this heretofore meek fellow hasn't shown, although Bert's no dummy. He knows where Mackie's headed, and it may be the best thing that's happened to him yet because he could skim this place 'til hell freezes over just so long as there's enough in the kitty not to raise suspicion and keep it humming. And what better partner to have?! Desperate people do desperate things. Bert just holds both hands as if *he's* being held up, smiling goofily. "Look, Ma! No hands!" And with a nifty kick of the plug with his left foot under the desk — Poof. No camera. Pointing now, with both hands still raised as if being held at gunpoint, his middle finger extended on each, pointing to the camera above. The camera's red light is off, and with a shit-eating grin on his face, we ain't never seen before, Bert's saying, "Now you see it, now you don't!" A cop, a clerk, and a kick of the security plug. "We're dark!"

Mackie acts impressed. "You are something else, ya know that, Bert? With stuff like that you shoulda been a magician!"

"I practiced magic as a kid, ya know."

"No, you never told me that. But I can believe it, I believe it. I knew it the moment I walked in here."

"Well...uh.... Look, officer."

"Dwayne."

"Officer Dwayne. I'll work with ya any way you want me to. I mean rooms are only going for $75 a night, though. But I'd be willing to—"

"No, no, now wait a minute Bert, wait. I don't want nothing from you. Honestly I don't. And I understand you ain't done nothing wrong."

"Yessir."

"In fact, nobody knows nothin', anyway. Right?" Mackie's pointing up at the camera. "All *I* wanna know is, what'd this guy look like?"

"Well, he was kinda...I dunno. Vanilla-looking. If you know what I mean."

"Not exactly."

"Well, what I mean is he was just a plain Jane."

"Gay huh."

"No, no. Nothing like that. Not that I know of anyway. Just what you'd say is 'nondescript.'"

"U-huh. How old would you say?"

"Late 50s maybe."

"How 'bout any distinguishing marks or anything like – scars, tattoos...."

"A mustache. He had a mustache. Just a regular vanilla mustache. Not a heavy one, kinda newish."

"White mustache."

"Black."

"Licorice."

"You got it."

"I'm gettin' hungry already, what else you got?"

• • •

Mackie sees through the translucent glass door that the Chief's on the phone, once again his feet kicked up on his desk. Just as he's hanging up, Mackie turns the knob. Caught off-guard, Chief's instinct is to reach for his gun as the door swings open. "Goddamn it, Mackie – don't you believe in fuckin' knockin'?!"

"I got 'em, Chief!"

"You got who? And next time knock, goddamn it! I almost reached for my fuckin' gun, dammit!"

"The sonofabitch who raped her."

"What sonofabitch who raped who? Who's been raped?" Mackie sits on the wooden chair opposite the Chief. "Make yourself at home why don't ya." Mackie instantly gets up. "Sit down goddamn it." Mackie sits.

"Chief. That woman was raped, for crissake, and we got the evidence to prove it."

"Mackie, now you gotta just calm down here. We ain't gonna get the lab results back for at least another week or two."

"I know. I know that, Chief, but I can prove who did it."

"Who did *what*?! She ain't even filed a rape claim."

"Well how can she claim somethin' when she don't even know who done it?"

"Well she can fuckin' say that, can't she!? She can say she was raped and she don't know who done it 'cause he was wearin' a gas mask or some other Halloween doodad. She ain't even said that much, right?!

Mackie has suddenly gone quiet. Chief's just looking at him, knowing he's come down pretty heavy, but there are lessons to be learned. Chief clearly has an affection for him, though. Chief's kind of subdued now. "You got a rape report from the hospital? Show it to me. C'mon – take it out. I wanna see it. We ain't got no rape report – not yet – we ain't got no DNA lab report – not yet-yet on that either, and I got a genius deputy sheriff here who can prove beyond a reasonable doubt that what nobody ever said happened, happened."

"But Chief–"

"Don't 'but Chief' me. 'Til she admits to something, we ain't got squat 'cause there ain't been no alleged crime filed. All we know is her husband died and she wigged out. *Okay!* And now she's a widow with a kid to take care of. *Okay!* on that, too – Now what?!"

Dejected, Mackie gets up to leave.

"Where're you goin'?" Mackie just gives a nod of *I dunno*. He's completely demoralized. "Mackie." He turns around now. Chief points him to sit down. "Talk to me."

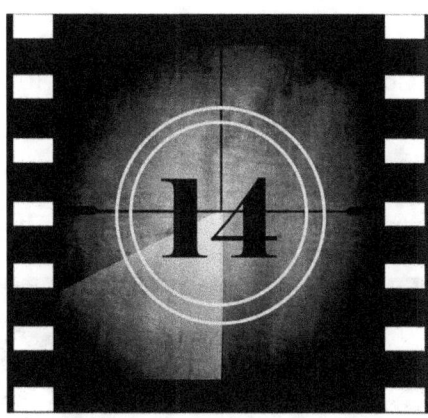

HIDDEN LAKE IS ABOUT A 20-MINUTE RIDE FROM EAST

Stroudsburg via Hollow Road.

It's a beautiful tranquil lake with plenty of rainbow trout and bass. We can see their rowboat in the distance now, just Danny and Uncle Joe. They're the only boat on the lake. And if you listen carefully, you might even hear Danny's shrieks of excitement – he's just landed a huge rainbow trout and Uncle Joe's helping him reel it in with a good-sized landing net at the ready. "Oh boy, Dan. This baby's huge. Let me help you with him, buddy. Looks like the whole camp's eatin' fish tonight!"

• • •

Meanwhile, the Chief's just winding up a call with Mary at the hospital and Mackie's still sitting there. "I see. She say where she was going?" Chief looks up at his wall clock. Almost five o'clock. "Uh-huh. So you figure they checked out 'bout half hour ago. Okay. Thank ya, Mary."

The Chief looks at Mackie. "They all left, sister picked her up. Mary thinks the doc and the kid went fishin'." A dirty-old-man grin steals over his face. "Wonder what the sister looks like." There's a moment of splendor on the Chief's face. But suddenly, reality strikes. "How in hell we gonna find where they are?" Mackie hasn't a clue. "DNA comes in and we're gonna be needin' to find her."

There's the longest pause.

"Wait a minute! Whatsamatter with me!" The Chief checks his numbers, picks up his phone and dials.

• • •

The rowboat in the middle of Hidden Lake has one gorgeous catch, so far, and it's Danny's. Meanwhile Joe's cell is ringing. He unlocks his black satchel. "This is Dr. Morris."

"Hate to be botherin' you like this, doc – this here's Chief Bowman."

"No bother at all, Chief. What can I help you with?"

"As if you ain't got enough to deal with, just that with your nephew up at the camp now, we gotta get contact info for next of kin, just in case of emergency an' stuff like that. I was wonderin' if I could get your sister's number where she'll be stayin.' But to be honest with you, doc, I'll be sure to call you first anyway."

Doctor Joe actually welcomes Chief Bowman being on top of this matter insofar as he's headed back into the city later tonight, with a book signing date tomorrow. "Sure thing, Chief. She's staying with Jamie, my other sister, at her place in Rhode Island for the next few weeks. In fact, if I can break away, I may pop up there over the weekend. Now hold on a second, Chief, Danny's literally rockin' the boat here. Looks like he's caught another one!"

Joe searches his cell for Jamie's number.

"He *did*?!" exclaims the Chief. "Well, you tell him to come by my office when he gets a chance and I'll make him an honorary deputy."

"Hey, Dan – Chief's gonna make you an honorary deputy. Whaddaya think of *that*!? Here's her number, Chief."

Danny's landed another huge rainbow trout. He's proud as a peacock. In fact, if Danny's ear-to-ear grin is any measure, the trout and the peacock are beginning to match!

"Here we go, Chief. Jamie's number is…."

• • •

Chief's phone is ringing again.

"Bowman here. Yeh, Bromide. "He *WHAT*?!" Whispers to Mackie, "Clarence gone shot himself in the head. Dead. No, no – do nothing. I'll call her myself."

• • •

We've seen these hands before. Bejeweled, bothered and bewildered. But something's missing. The hand now is not the hand of Margaret. There's only the gold wedding band; she had many more. Gently, Marvin lowers the stylus onto the record. Somebody must've dropped it though; the crack is hair thin and barely playable, though playable still.

• • •

> *"Long years have past now, I never wed.*
> *True to my first love, though she is dead.*
> *She tried to tell me, tried to explain—*
> *I would not listen, pleadings were vain.*
> *One day a letter came from the man;*
> *he was her brother, the letter ran.*
> *That's why I'm lonely, no home at all—*
> *I broke her heart, pet, after the ball."*

• • •

DENOUEMENT

He is holding a match to the corner of the 5x7 B&W photograph of two twenty-somethings in the Fun House Hall of Mirrors: the selfie he took of Margie and himself, who, though we never met Margie, was Clarence's mother. He gently lights the corner of the picture with a match…and before his eyes, and ours, the past slowly and forever disappears.

He's bald now, but we knew that, standing in front of the blazing fire, dressed like the man he never really was, in the very suit he'd worn at the ball…those many years ago.

Our Maine coon, foreseeing the outcome, (as some have been known to do), awakens from the comfort of her slumber, speaks a bit (harshly at that), jumps onto the vanity, knocking down the remaining mementos of time, and leaves.

His head bowed, the flames engulf his fingers, as happiness burns in his hand. The tip of his jacket has caught a flame; the fabric will take its own good time. The mannequins are bare of wigs, no pink duvet. The fireplace has it all now.

He stands now in effigy of himself.

It's getting late.

• • •

"Hey, Dan – whaddaya say we head back to camp. Wait'll Uncle Bob and all the kids see what you caught. And remember, I got the cell shots to prove it."

"Cool."

Danny and Uncle Joe, having just paid the Boat & Tackle guy, walk back towards the car. Danny's got his red Tesla Roadster in hand. He ain't letting *that* out of his sight, no how! Besides which, you know he's going to show it off to the other kids anyway. So between his Tesla in one hand, and two trouts in the other, and pictures to prove it—*for all time*—Liza will be awed.

At the end of the path is the real deal. While Joe continues to walk towards it, Danny just stands there, mesmerized. The model in his hand is literally parked in front of him. Suddenly realizing that Danny's still standing there, Joe turns towards him. "Whatsa matter, Dan? It's still the same car we came up in, partner." Joe realizes the passion he feels for this, just as Marvin loved his camera. Danny stands transfixed. "You like it that much, huh?"

Moist-eyed, Danny nods yes.

"Well, c'mon – someday you'll have one of your own. 'Xcept by then it'll drive itself on even longer trips."

"That's no fun, Uncle Joe. *I* wanna drive it."

"Well, you will. It's just that you'll have more options." Danny gets in on the passenger side as Joe takes Danny's model Roadster and puts it on the seat in back, moving his open satchel briefcase in the process.

"Ya know, Uncle Joe, Google's got cars that drive themselves."

"I think they even got em that fly now, too, you know," says Joe. "You'll see, you'll be flying and driving all at the same time. Like I said, it'll all be waiting there for you, Dan."

Joe bends over now to buckle Danny's seat belt, first. Danny just looks at him. "Uncle Joe?" Joe looks at him. "I love you, Uncle Joe."

Joe Morris seems genuinely touched. "I love you too, Danny."

"I wish you were my daddy."

Again Joe looks at him. There's a moment of quiet. Joe tousles his hair. Nods an understanding—the message: *so do I*. Dr. Morris opens the glove compartment, tosses Danny a pair of driving gloves, while taking a pair for himself. "Okay, pardner, suit up! Seat belt in place?!"

"YUP!"

• • •

"You know," says Chief Bowman, "I ain't never even seen this Sally woman. She potent?"

"Oh man. Gorgeous," says Mackie.

"You don't say."

"And I seen her in a *bad* way."

"I'll be damned. You see her sister, too?"

"Nope."

"You don't say. How many sisters you figure he's got?"

"Tell ya the truth Chief, I'm not sure."

"Hmph. I'll be damned." Mackie's got Dr. Morris' paperback sitting on the desk there. "You still reading his book? I thought you finished it. Let me see that thing." Mackie just pushes it his way.

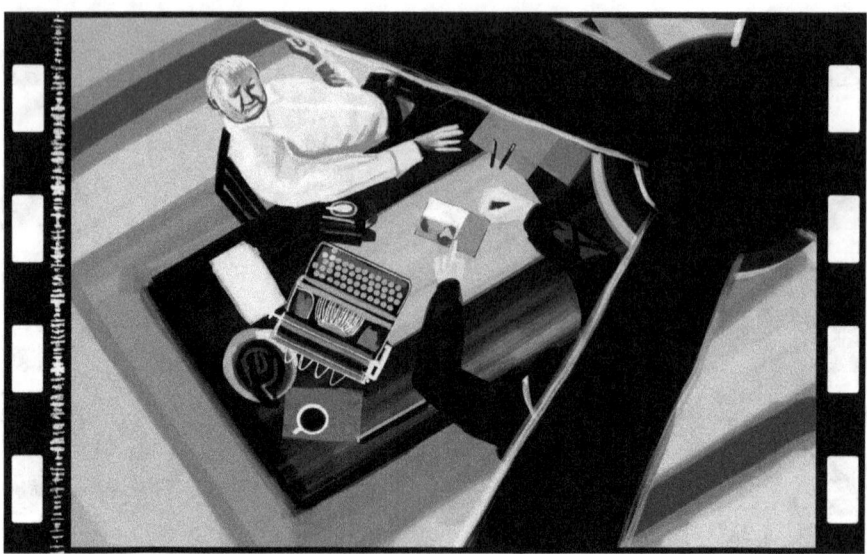

Chief reaches in and turns it over to its front cover.

"*Multiple Personality Disorders* by Joseph E. Morris, MD and Psychiatrist." Chief turns it back over again. He's looking at the photo of the younger Joseph Morris. Vaguely familiar, perhaps, even to our eyes. 'Famed author and authority.' I'll be damned."

SLOW FADE OUT.

AFTERWORD
"JUST THE FACTS, MA'AM"
Det. Joe Friday—"Dragnet"

Dear Reader:

HERE ARE SOME ANSWERS TO QUESTIONS I POSED TO Dr. Lawrence Kobilinsky, Professor Emeritus of Forensic Science at John Jay College of Criminal Justice, The City University of New York.

It occurred to me that you might have some lingering questions of your own, given some open-ended issues in the story itself. Though we cannot say it in provable scientific terms quite yet, we pretty much know Whodunit. But "Pretty much know" wouldn't've cut it for Chief Bowman! So we'll wait and see what comes back.

Marvin and Clarence, on the other hand, could never have been 100% certain of anything. We do have Marvin's story, though – even some framed photos to go with it - and the letter he received from Margie's brother, so long, long ago, which I was inclined to believe. But Clarence's deeply felt conviction, which he tried to give voice to but couldn't, gives pause. I somehow suspect he knew a truth he kept even from me.

Sometimes in life there are no good answers.

Joe J.

AUTHOR'S FOLLOW-UP:

FROM: Dr. Lawrence Kobilinsky

TO: Joseph Jacoby

Once a crime is reported to the police, especially a crime like rape, police will investigate.

At the scene, police will contact the Evidence Collection Team and the scene is photographed and evidence collected, packaged and vouchered. This evidence is sent to the property clerk's office.

The victim is brought to the emergency room for a rape kit (Sexual Offence Evidence Collection Kit) to be completed. If the victim has demonstrated signs of emotional trauma, a referral is made to a hospital psychiatrist. Generally, hospital psychiatrists are not brought into the matter unless the ER doctor deems it necessary i.e. nervous breakdown.

After sampling is finished the rape kit is turned over to the police and it is vouchered and stored in the property clerk's office temporarily. Ultimately, rape kit evidence is sent to the medical examiner.

I do not know if it is incumbent on police to inform the victim about the name of the perpetrator. The case is reported to the DA's office by the police department and a prosecutor is assigned to work with police and OCME.[1]

AUTHOR'S SUMMATION

Given our particular situation here with Sally, when the DNA results come back from the OCME, the local authorities will have a match between the Motel key and the floating condom, as well as with the physical description of the suspect that was given to Officer Mackie by the Motel Manager.

. . . .

[1] The Office of Chief Medical Examiner

Going now on a very strong circumstantial hunch, the police will attempt to get a cup or bottle he drank from.

If and when a definite match is obtained between all of the samples, the Assistant District Attorney is the individual who will approach Sally with the State's conclusions and legal case.

Sally will be offered the opportunity to bear witness on the stand for rape. That will be her decision to make.

A DA will not pursue a case without a complainant in most instances. It is as if the rape victim says it was consensual.

• • •

MORE QUESTIONS...

Question:
If a rape case goes to trial and is upheld what would be the likely punishment?

Dr. Kobilinsky:
It varies, but for first-degree rape it can be imprisonment for up to 25 years. Usual minimum sentence is 5 years. But there is plea-bargaining and mitigating circumstance that comes into sentencing.

Question:
Would you guess that some women would rather live in doubt than find out who her rapist was?

Dr. Kobilinsky:
Hard call here: A woman is raped and does not know who did it. Presumably she wants to know who did it and that justice will be meted out in a courtroom. Why would she not want to know? If it turns out that it is her brother, then that becomes a double whammy for her.

Question:

Is there lasting emotional trauma from sibling rape?

Dr. Kobilinsky:

Without a doubt! Psychiatric help is in order.

Question:

How prevalent is sibling rape in the U.S.?

Dr. Kobilinsky:

Check Wikipedia. My own hunch is that it is less than 1%. I also think that valid statistics are not known.

• • •

WITH REGARD TO MARVIN AND CLARENCE...

Question:

What would have been the earliest possible year that a person could have done a DNA test with an infant to determine parentage?

Dr. Kobilinsky:

1985-1986 in England using RFLP. 1990 in the States using PCR.[2]

Question:

A) In your experience, if a man suspects that his fiancé (whom he never married) had an affair, and does not know if the child is his or not **(but raised him after she died in childbirth)**, is he likely to do DNA Testing later?

. . . .

[2] What is the difference between RFLP and PCR?
RFLP allows identifying DNA fragments based on unique patterns of restriction enzyme cutting in specific regions of DNA and seeing them in gel. Whereas, Real time PCR, is an amplification of your target gene using specific primers, and you can monitor the reaction in real time.

Dr. Kobilinsky:

Probably not.

> B) Would he need her consent to do DNA testing whether or not he is listed as the birth father?

Dr. Kobilinsky:

He would not need any consent to do DNA testing on the child.

Question:

Given the 40-odd year passage of time, is this something her then-fiancé would still want to have answers to, do you think – or better to let sleeping dogs lie?

Dr. Kobilinsky:

Dogs like to sleep. Let them sleep.

Question:

Is infant DNA any different from adult DNA? Does it change in any way? The reason I ask: Since the child was born prior to 1985, and given that the rapist may have also committed the first rape of her older sister (now deceased), notwithstanding his denials in a letter to her fiancé, would the DNA still match the 40 year-old male child if the child was his.

Dr. Kobilinsky:

An infant's DNA will remain the same throughout his lifetime. So that as an adult, it will remain identical. Remember that a child has half of the father's DNA. Same for the mother.

Question:

When we get full confirmation of his DNA profile, and if her brother had earlier raped their deceased sister, will that be provable?

Dr. Kobilinsky:

Here are the facts as you describe below:

1. The eldest sister MAY have had a child with the brother (shrink).

2. The child was brought up by Marvin as his own.

3. The younger sister, Sally, was raped by the brother but is not pressing charges.

4. Can it be shown that the child who was brought up by Marvin is the child of the brother and the eldest sister who is deceased?

The answer is yes but it is complicated. It is complicated because the child may be the product of an incestual relationship. Brother and his sister/lover share half of their genes, and child gets half his genes from each parent. At the same time, the two sisters share half of their genes with each other and one sister (possible mother) is deceased and not testable.

If the police/OCME DNA analysts have been looking at the rape evidence, then they know the DNA profile of Sally and the Brother. But nobody knows the profile of the eldest deceased sister, (possible mother of the child).

This makes the analysis somewhat more complex but it can certainly be determined if the child was fathered by the brother.

GENESIS OF THIS BOOK

WHEN I WAS A KID GROWING UP IN BROOKLYN,
I fell in love with the movies. My mother took me to them whenever
she could. But it never occurred to me, as a 6-year-old, that movies were
conscious constructs, planned out in advance, with actors following lines
already written. And behind-the-camera was a Director and dozens of
technicians who made up the team that got a movie made. As I sat in that
darkened movie theater, everything up on that screen was real. But even
if I'd realized it was 'put together' for an audience, I'd have pushed that
aside; it wouldn't have mattered. Movies were prototypes of worlds to
come for anyone who subscribed.

That big screen was the window onto these worlds. And for me, happier ones than the one I knew outside (besides, on *sunny* days, I always got a headache when I left the movie theater and went outside). I never understood, though, why Fred Astaire was such a big movie star. He was kinda skinny and his voice was high-pitched. But I made the adjustments. Adjustments were things I was good at. For the record, though, when I grew up I changed my mind about Fred Astaire.

And then there were the Saturday Matinees and Looney Tunes. And when *they* started running, they just *kept* on running, one right after another, and I didn't want them to *stop* running, and so I "willed it" that they'd *keep* running. *Ten* I counted! I was convinced it was personal; that I'd somehow affected an outcome. You can say the movies became "interactive" for me long before we had such a word (and I'm not so sure I got it wrong, either).

When I looked up at the ceiling in the movie theater, and saw that beam of light being projected from the booth way up in the back, above the balcony even, I'd made up my mind to get up there someday. To my way of thinking, that's where all the magic came from. How it got there I don't think I ever gave much thought to. Not *Yet*. Whoever was up there, though, was putting on the show and I wanted to put on the show. And that beam of light over my head, with all those dust particles swirling around inside it, made its way onto the big white screen and another world.

Meanwhile, though, I had to figure a way to make my own movies without a camera, or projector. My mother bought me a sheet of white oak tag and 8.5 x 11 paper, crayons, scotch tape and a scissor - and I was on my way as a moviemaker, theater owner, projectionist, and even the audience, all in one (I almost forgot 'actor').

The fact that I had no story to tell, and couldn't draw a straight line, didn't matter. I was always good with titles, though, and I knew the last frame of the film because I'd seen it at the movies - *The End*. All I needed now was the stuff in the middle. The important thing was to make something up and get on with the show. And with the putting together of the show, I forgot all about the present; my imagined "reality" was far better than anything I'd ever known, anyway.

On the next sheet of 8.5x11, I drew something with my crayons, which, even if I'd saved the stuff, I wouldn't have been able to decipher today, anyway, and probably couldn't have done it then either, even if I'd run the show only once. This was not Infantile Alzheimer's. It's just that *everything* came and went. And some of it went even before it came.

Some shrink might've figured it out, though. Anything's possible. Chances are excellent he'd have come up with a lot better story than anything I coulda dreamt up. All I was interested in was getting to *The End*. Success!

So I scotch-taped the Title sheet to the next sheet, and so on and so forth, and I could feel it building. The mechanics of putting this together was exciting, and I must've been talking to myself about some kind of story (something I still do) and between the two of me, the story took hold. And before I knew it...*The End*.

The white sheet of oak tag was my movie screen. I cut two vertical slits for the scenes to be able to be pulled through. I was really putting together a slide show, but I didn't think of it that way because there was movement in *my* mind as I did it, and movement was the *essential* ingredient of a movie, and surprise, too, because you never knew what was coming next - not even me. And then, *The End*. But I very much doubt, that had I put this show on more than once, I'd have ever come up with the same story twice.

As an adult, when I actually did get to make my first picture, I would pitch the storyline to individual investors (without a screenplay), but each time I pitched it, the story changed. I wasn't actually aware of this until my attorney, one day, made a stunning observation: We were on the bus going to meet some prospective investors. I had thanked Jack for coming to these 'pitches' (free of charge) and lending his credibility to my credibility, and he just laughed out loud and said: "Are you kidding? I *love* coming to these meetings just to hear you tell the story - you never tell the same story twice!" By now, though, I was in my mid-20s. Without even thinking about it, I was up to my old tricks. Whatever you needed to hear, I'd fill it in.

It worked.

• • •

The reason I've been telling you this is because, while I have since learned that you'd better tell the story first and make the drawings after, it occurred to me that what I was doing here is precisely what I did as a kid: Making movies without a camera. Only this time with the story written out first. And the pictures, second. And *you're* the projectionist, pulling it along at your own pace, without the crayons (unless you wanna color them in).

Hope you enjoyed the show.

Tell your friends.

Joe J.
Storyteller and Co-Projectionist.

ABOUT THE AUTHOR

JOSEPH JACOBY, screenwriter/author, director-producer, began his career as a creator of game shows and as a puppeteer. He has written-directed 5 motion pictures to date. His first theatrical feature, *Shame, Shame...Everybody Knows Her Name,* was made a permanent part of the Museum of Modern Art's film collection. In 2006, MoMA mounted a weeklong retrospective of his film work, coinciding with the publication of his first book, a memoir, *Boy On A String,* with an Introduction by Martin Scorsese. He was the recipient of the "Best New Director" award at the Virgin Islands Film Festival for *The Great Bank Hoax* (Warner Bros.) and honored for the picture at The Festival De Deauville Du Cinema Americain. His original family Musical, *Davy Jones' Locker,* starring the famed Bil Baird Marionettes, was the recipient of the Gold Award at Worldfest Houston and awarded the UNIMA-USA Citation of Excellence in the Art of Puppetry by The American Center of the Union Internationale de la Marionette, founded by Jim Henson. His documentary, *A Case of MisTaken Identity?* was seen nationally on the PBS stations in 2008-09. In December 2009, *The New York Times* reprinted its film critic's reviews, citing 3 of the best independent pictures of the 70s, including Jacoby's second feature, *Hurry Up, Or I'll Be 30,* featuring Danny DeVito in his first theatrical film performance. Jacoby lives in New York City.

JosephJacoby.com

www.ingramcontent.com/pod-product-compliance
Lightning Source LLC
Chambersburg PA
CBHW071117100726
47908CB00008B/2400